The City of Conversation

Anthony Giardina

A SAMUEL FRENCH ACTING EDITION

FOUNDED 1830

SAMUELFRENCH.COM
SAMUELFRENCH-LONDON.CO.UK

FOR PRODUCTION ENQUIRIES

UNITED STATES AND CANADA
Info@SamuelFrench.com
1-866-598-8449

UNITED KINGDOM AND EUROPE
Plays@SamuelFrench-London.co.uk
020-7255-4302

Each title is subject to availability from Samuel French, depending upon country of performance. Please be aware that *THE CITY OF CONVERSATION* may not be licensed by Samuel French in your territory. Professional and amateur producers should contact the nearest Samuel French office or licensing partner to verify availability.

MUSIC USE NOTE

Licensees are solely responsible for obtaining formal written permission from copyright owners to use copyrighted music in the performance of this play and are strongly cautioned to do so. If no such permission is obtained by the licensee, then the licensee must use only original music that the licensee owns and controls. Licensees are solely responsible and liable for all music clearances and shall indemnify the copyright owners of the play(s) and their licensing agent, Samuel French, against any costs, expenses, losses and liabilities arising from the use of music by licensees. Please contact the appropriate music licensing authority in your territory for the rights to any incidental music.

IMPORTANT BILLING AND CREDIT REQUIREMENTS

If you have obtained performance rights to this title, please refer to your licensing agreement for important billing and credit requirements.

THE CITY OF CONVERSATION was first produced by the Lincoln Center Theater (André Bishop, Producing Artistic Director; Adam Siegel, Managing Director) at the Mitzi E. Newhouse Theater in New York City on April 10, 2014. The performance was directed by Doug Hughes, with sets by John Lee Beatty, costumes by Catherine Zuber, lighting by Tyler Micoleau, and original music and sound by Mark Bennett. The Production Stage Manager was James FitzSimmons. The cast was as follows:

JEAN SWIFT	Beth Dixon
COLIN FERRIS/ETHAN FERRIS (AGE 27)	Michael Simpson
ANNA FITZGERALD	Kristen Bush
HESTER FERRIS	Jan Maxwell
GEORGE MALLONEE	John Aylward
CHANDLER HARRIS	Kevin O'Rourke
CAROLYN MALLONEE	Barbara Garrick
ETHAN FERRIS (AGE 6)	Luke Niehaus
DONALD LOGAN	Phillip James Brannon

CHARACTERS

JEAN SWIFT
COLIN FERRIS
ANNA FITZGERALD
HESTER FERRIS
GEORGE MALLONEE
CHANDLER HARRIS
CAROLYN MALLONEE
ETHAN FERRIS, at age 6
ETHAN FERRIS, at age 27
DONALD LOGAN

ETHAN and COLIN can be, and are intended to be, played by the same actor.

SETTING

The living room of a townhouse in Georgetown, in Washington, D.C.

TIME

Fall 1979 to January 2009

AUTHOR'S NOTES

A note on the use of parentheses in dialogue: when a line begins or ends with certain words enclosed in parentheses, it means that the words are meant to overlap with the words in the following or preceding parentheses. In other words, those are places where people are meant to deliberately step on each other's lines.

ACT ONE

Scene One

(October, 1979.)

(In the dark, we hear excerpts from Jimmy Carter's 1979 "Malaise" speech – "The erosion of our confidence in the future is threatening to destroy the social and political fabric of America... The symptoms of this crisis of the American spirit are all around us... Washington D.C. has become an island. The gap between our our citizens and government has never been so wide.")

(Lights come up on a living room in Georgetown. The room is well appointed, not extravagant. There should be very small signs of eccentric taste. On a credenza, an array of small framed photographs. Large windows open onto the top of a garden. Doors stage right open onto a kitchen (unseen); there is an entrance to the dining room at lower stage right. Stairs lead to a bedroom upstairs.)

(JEAN SWIFT is seated at a small table, eating from a plate of toast. It is mid-morning. She has a list in front of her, and is checking things off, making notes. She has reading glasses on, and is dressed neatly. She is in her mid-fifties.)

HESTER. *(calls from upstairs)* Cream of tartar? Jean? Do we have some? The caterer (asked especially) –

JEAN. (In the lazy Susan.) There should be plenty.

HESTER. Would you look? Would you make sure?

JEAN. *(wanting to finish her toast)* Hester, tell her you'll call her back.

HESTER. She says she'll hold.

JEAN. *(affected pique, as she rises, wipes her mouth with a napkin, goes into the kitchen)* I'll go.

*(As soon as **JEAN** exits, **COLIN** and **ANNA** enter from downstage. They are in their late twenties, wearing backpacks, and carrying one shared suitcase. They look exhausted, not particularly clean. **COLIN**'s hair is longish; he may have a bit of a beard. They wear the clothes of ex-hippies of the period – jeans, perhaps corduroy jackets (much worn). **ANNA**'s hair is long and blonde; she wears very high, attention-getting boots.)*

COLIN. The remains of a Spartan breakfast. Welcome to Washington, D.C.

*(He eats the rest of **JEAN**'s toast.)*

ANNA. *(at the window)* I like the view.

COLIN. You'll like it even more. Joseph Alsop's house is over there. My mother will tell you all about it. The famous dinner she attended there with Jack Kennedy. Aren't you hungry?

ANNA. Starved.

COLIN. Here.

*(They share the last piece of toast. A sexy little moment between them as **COLIN** feeds her.)*

My mother lives to tell this story. The night in 1962 when Kennedy showed up for dinner looking all troubled until he saw, across the room, Isaiah Berlin.

(A beat.)

There won't be more of this, you know.

*(to **ANNA**'s silent question:)*

My mother doesn't believe in keeping food in the house.

ANNA. I'll be fine. Just need a nap, that's all. And a shower.

*(**JEAN** enters from the kitchen, holding a cup of coffee, calling up to **HESTER**.)*

JEAN. Hester, I took it down –

(Shocked at the sight of COLIN *and* ANNA, *she nearly drops her coffee.)*

COLIN. Hold on.

JEAN. Colin, we didn't expect you until (tomorrow*).*

COLIN. (Hold on.) Let me take your coffee. Give you a hug.

JEAN. *(as he hugs her, hard, lifting her off her feet)* Big boy. Oh my Lord.

COLIN. You didn't expect me until tomorrow because my mother got it wrong. Didn't she?

JEAN. Yes. No. She said – your letter said –

COLIN. Today. My letter said today. No matter. This is – (I'd like you to meet)

JEAN. (But she's having a) dinner tonight. Oh, you look wonderful. Scruffy, but healthy.

COLIN. My aunt Jean, I'd like you to meet Anna Fitzgerald.

JEAN. I'm sorry. Of course.

(She regards ANNA*'s boots.)*

Welcome. I'm the aunt.

ANNA. Yes. (Nice to –)

COLIN. (A dinner) for who?

JEAN. Senator Mallonee from Kentucky. I'll call her. She'll be furious with herself.

(out of the side of her mouth, as if being mock-private)

In curlers.

(calling, as she goes upstairs:)

Hester! Colin's home a day early!

COLIN. *(calling after her)* I'm not – home – a day –

(Giving up, he turns, and he and ANNA *smile at one another.)*

She loved your boots.

ANNA. I noticed.

COLIN. Washington is not about boots like that.

ANNA. Not yet, anyway.

COLIN. *(made slightly nervous by what ANNA's just said, he calls off:)* Jean, is there more toast?

JEAN. *(re-enters)* She's coming, she's coming. Of course she doesn't want you to see her in curlers. But she's so excited.

(As COLIN holds up the plate expectantly:)

No, I'm afraid not. You know how she is. I brought my own from home. I'll see if there's something in the cupboards. They didn't feed you on the plane?

(heading back into the kitchen)

Hester, never mind the curlers! Colin is dying to see you!

(As JEAN heads into the kitchen, HESTER enters. She is in a silk robe, hurriedly taking curlers out of her hair, holding a hairbrush. In spite of the fact that we are not seeing her at her best, it is evident that she is a glamorous woman with a vivid sensuality. Like her sister, she is in her early fifties, and very excited to see her son.)

HESTER. Darling. You were supposed to arrive tomorrow.

COLIN. Today, actually.

HESTER. No, I was sure. You're positively hirsute. Cave man. Oh God, you're gorgeous, though.

(The following line should be said as they engage in a huge hug.)

How dare you come and see me when I'm like this? Curlers in my hair.

(Within the hug, she regards ANNA.)

Who's this?

COLIN. I wrote you. Do you read my letters? Anna Fitzgerald, my mother. Hester Ferris.

(As JEAN did, HESTER regards ANNA's boots with a barely disguised critical regard.)

HESTER. My son is a terrible correspondent.

ANNA. I know.

HESTER. Forgive me.

ANNA. His scrawl is unreadable. Don't blame yourself.

HESTER. I don't. It's very nice to meet you, though. Unprepared as I am.

ANNA. *(slightly intimidated, in spite of her attempt not to be)*
I've seen pictures of you looking extraordinarily glamorous. So there's no need to apologize for the curlers.

HESTER. Thank you. That's kind. Where did you find her, Colin? Did you attend the London School of Economics as well?

ANNA. I did.

COLIN. Winner of the Ormsby Prize.

HESTER. My.

ANNA. *(deflecting attention from herself)* With Henry Kissinger.

(In response to **HESTER***'s slight confusion:)*

The picture I'm talking about. You at Nixon's Second Inaugural. The dress you wore.

HESTER. That was ages ago. Seven years, I think. But thank you.

*(*JEAN *enters, holding a box of Pop Tarts.)*

JEAN. Here. Will this do? I think you toast them.

COLIN. Aunt Jean, check the expiration date.

*(*JEAN *puts on her glasses, does.)*

JEAN. Oh dear.

(She exits.)

COLIN. *(He puts his hands around his mother's face, squeezing maybe a little too roughly.)*
Do you throw nothing out? Do you buy nothing new?

HESTER. Don't. Dear.

COLIN. Why not? Mess with you?

(touching her face more affectionately, almost sexually, now)

Can't mess with you?

HESTER. Of course you can. But my face has become so vulnerable. And tonight, Senator Mallonee is coming.

*(**HESTER** has by now begun removing her curlers, and will, throughout the remainder of the scene, begin brushing her hair, to bring herself to her customary level of presentableness.)*

COLIN. To dinner. I know.

HESTER. With his wife. From Kentucky.

COLIN. Well, what are you worried about? Not enough chairs? Last time I was in the dining room I counted six. And we can bring an extra one in for Jean.

HESTER. Oh, Jean doesn't come to these dinners. You know that. Now stop joking with me. This is important. You have to promise to behave.

COLIN. Of course I will.

HESTER. Promise. Don't sass him. This is hugely important.

COLIN. You can give us some money and send us out for something to eat and have us arrive just in time to say goodbye.

HESTER. I want you here.

COLIN. *(to **ANNA**)* What she used to do.

HESTER. But I want you to look nice. Will you do me the biggest favor and get a haircut?

COLIN. Why?

HESTER. Because these are conservative people, Colin, and you've been away. Sideburns are fine. Sideburns are in fact disgustingly fashionable in this town right now. But long hair is not –

COLIN. Not what?

HESTER. It brings back memories. Raw – things. Vietnam. We're barely over Vietnam here. I'm sure in London it's all ancient history. I can have Chandler make you an appointment in the Congressional barber shop.

COLIN. What's this dinner about? Excuse me –

*(turning to **ANNA**)*

Dinner, you have to understand, is always about something.

HESTER. It's really all settled. It's a little Judiciary Committee thing.

JEAN. *(enters, holding a plate)* I found an egg. And scrambled it.

COLIN. God bless you, Aunt Jean.

(Ravenous, he eats.)

JEAN. One lone egg in the back of the refrigerator.

COLIN. *(remembering to offer some of the egg to* ANNA, *who refuses it)* So. Judiciary Committee thing.

HESTER. Chandler and Teddy Kennedy. And you won't believe it – even Strom Thurmond has signed on. It all started when Jimmy Carter –

COLIN. *(to* ANNA, *explaining, and hugely amused by his mother's opinions)* The unforgivable one.

HESTER. President Seatwarmer. The Emperor of Malaise. Appointed a federal judge by all accounts decent except that he refuses to resign from his all-white country club.

COLIN. Aunt Jean, this is the Willie Mays of eggs.

JEAN. *(flattered)* There was only one.

COLIN. Yes. Go on.

HESTER. It's something Chandler and Teddy are trying to do. Force resignations.

COLIN. From all-white country clubs.

HESTER. As a kind of benchmark for nomination to the Federal judiciary. Which of course should have happened years ago. Should have happened. But well, now, Teddy, Chandler, Strom Thurmond –

COLIN. And hopefully Senator Mallonee from Kentucky.

HESTER. Which is an awful state. You know that.

COLIN. *(starting off)* I'm going to wash this plate, Aunt Jean. So you don't have to. And then stow some of this stuff.

JEAN. Oh no, you shouldn't have to (wash it) –

COLIN. Why is Kentucky an awful state?

HESTER. Think about it. Who ever has come from Kentucky?

COLIN. The Great Compromiser, Henry Clay. Zachary Taylor. Lincoln was raised there.

HESTER. You're so good.

COLIN. Do you think I've forgotten all those dinnertime tutorials? Other kids got "Pat the Bunny". I got selections from de Tocqueville.

(He exits, with his and **ANNA**'s *bags. Both* **HESTER** *and* **JEAN** *smile after him, appreciating him.)*

JEAN. He shouldn't have to wash it.

(She exits after **COLIN**. **HESTER** *and* **ANNA** *are alone.* **HESTER** *has by now removed all her rollers and is brushing her hair.)*

HESTER. Anna Fitzgerald.

ANNA. Yes. From Minneapolis. Obsequious Minneapolis.

HESTER. I'll bet you're an ambitious girl.

ANNA. I'll bet you're right.

HESTER. Come to look around Washington?

ANNA. Yes. To see if it's the place. To see if it's the right fit.

HESTER. Colin should know that. He grew up here.

ANNA. But I didn't...

HESTER. And you're that kind of couple. It has to work for both of you.

ANNA. Yes.

HESTER. Dual careers. Parallel tracks.

ANNA. Yes. I wonder if I could ask you something.

(A beat. **HESTER** *nods permission.)*

Something arising out of my naivete. My Minneapolisness.

HESTER. Of course.

ANNA. Can I watch you get ready?

*(***HESTER** *tilts her head. It's an odd request.)*

Watch how you do it. How you choose what to wear. How you – stage yourself. I'd like to learn.

HESTER. I think I saw this movie.

(Now it's ANNA's turn to tilt her head, not sure where this is leading.)

The young faux-naif making up to the aging star.

(ANNA still doesn't seem to get it.)

It's called *All About Eve.*

ANNA. Forgive me. I didn't want to make that kind of impression.

HESTER. But you have. All right. First lesson. Washington is about boldness, but it has to be couched in layers. People smell ambition. They do, and they defend themselves. The turf is not so large, you know.

COLIN. *(enters, angry)* Jesus, he's got his stuff all over my room. Where exactly are we supposed to sleep?

HESTER. Who? Who's got his stuff?

COLIN. Chandler. You've allowed him to take over.

HESTER. Well, I let him use your room, of course, but I didn't know he had "taken over".

COLIN. Don't you two sleep together?

HESTER. What a question.

COLIN. Well, why does he need two rooms?

HESTER. Jean will clean it up. Jean!

COLIN. She's your sister. She's not the maid.

(The next four lines should overlap one another:)

HESTER. *(calling offstage)* Jean! will you take Chandler's things out of Colin's room?

JEAN. *(offstage)* And put them where?

HESTER. In mine.

COLIN. Jean. No. I will do it.

(turning to his mother:)

Why in God's name don't you two just get married?

HESTER. Because we can't. You know that. He's married. You know that.

COLIN. I'm surprised you're not afraid of being found out. You and the senior Senator from Virginia.

HESTER. Darling, it's still a small town in one sense. When you find yourself seated next to Don Graham at dinner every two weeks or so, you don't have to worry about your affairs turning up in the Washington Post.

COLIN. *(to* **ANNA**, *another demonstration of what he's wanted to show her)* You see? Everything covered.

(It's only now that he picks up on the tension between these two women.)

What – happened?

ANNA. Nothing.

HESTER. Nothing at all. One little mistake.

(She's now almost over-friendly to **ANNA***, perhaps even taking her hand.)*

You get more than one mistake, Anna. Listen. I have a dress for tonight I think you'd look splendid in.

ANNA. I have a dress.

HESTER. No, no, let me do this, to make up for being a little too harsh with you before. Please. That dress you spoke about before, from Nixon's Inaugural – I still have it. I've saved it, of course I've saved it.

(calling off)

Jean, the black Geoffrey Beene in the back of my closet! I'm sure you'll be able to get into it. Please. Let me.

(She exits.)

ANNA. She's very good.

COLIN. Oh, she's the best but you're her match. Trust me.

*(**COLIN** approaches her from behind, lifts up her hair, tickles the back of her neck.)*

Listen, don't lose your nerve tonight.

ANNA. In her dress.

COLIN. Wear the dress. You don't have a dress as good as hers. Dazzle them tonight. Wear the dress.

(JEAN *enters, carrying the dress, followed by* HESTER.)

JEAN. I think this should fit you nicely.

HESTER. Try it on.

(ANNA *takes the dress and starts to move off.*)

Where are you going?

ANNA. To try it on.

HESTER. Dear, you don't need privacy. We're all women. Except for Colin.

JEAN. And he's seen you, no doubt.

ANNA. Yes. He has.

HESTER. Try it on.

ANNA. I'd prefer privacy.

COLIN. There's a bathroom right off the hallway.

HESTER. *(as* ANNA *is exiting)* Just – leave the boots here, dear.

(ANNA *is half shocked, half amused by this. She takes the boots off, then exits. As soon as she's gone,* HESTER *picks up the boots as though she's handling something rancid, and places them beside what we presume to be a door downstage.*)

COLIN. What exactly are you doing?

HESTER. You can't be serious about that girl.

COLIN. I am entirely serious about that girl.

HESTER. She'll eat you alive. I have an instinct about these things.

JEAN. Hester.

COLIN. Then I'll be eaten alive. I'm going to marry her.

(*This affects* HESTER *more than she'd like to show.*)

JEAN. That's wonderful.

HESTER. Colin, I am sure you're utterly enchanted, as who wouldn't be? That hair and those legs. But you don't marry a girl like that.

COLIN. No? I thought you did. I thought you fall in love with a girl like that and the next most natural thing in the world was to want to spend your life with her.

HESTER. You want to have a career here, don't you?

COLIN. Here. Or somewhere.

HESTER. Don't be silly. Who do you think you're talking to? She's come here so that she can take over this town. You'll be her little adjunct.

COLIN. We both did well. Stars, you might say. At the London School of Economics.

HESTER. Well, let me call up Cy Vance right now and tell him that. Because of course that doesn't make you a dime a dozen in this town.

COLIN. All right. Enough.

HESTER. I had looked forward to having you here.

(JEAN *looks at the floor, embarrassed.* **COLIN** *notices this.*)

COLIN. To groom me. To make sure I don't put a foot wrong.

HESTER. Say it that way if you must.

(ANNA *enters, looking spectacular in the dress.*)

I knew it!

JEAN. Stunning.

HESTER. You're transformed.

ANNA. Am I?

HESTER. Senator Mallonee will have eyes for no one else.

ANNA. Well.

HESTER. Though there are always rumors about him playing for the other team.

(**COLIN** *and* **ANNA** *look at her, questioning.*)

Well, he is a conservative Republican, after all.

JEAN. Paging Noël Coward.

(*They all look at* **JEAN**. *She smiles to herself.*)

HESTER. But tonight, seeing you in this dress, he will be entirely and forcefully heterosexual. And now let me tell you why it's so important that you both of you – please just be decorative and gentle at dinner.

The stakes are huge for us tonight. Teddy needs us to secure this vote so he can start off his Presidential campaign with a bang. And if Chandler can do this for Teddy, there's a very good chance he'll have a shot at the Cabinet, or even the Vice Presidency. I'm being quite naked about this in order to ask you this hugely important favor.

COLIN. We're going to be half asleep at the dinner table. I don't think you have to worry about us being anything but –

ANNA. Decorative and gentle.

HESTER. And a haircut, please?

(COLIN *shakes his head.*)

This is important, Colin. It's important to Chandler.

COLIN. *(starting off)* I'm going to clear out Chandler's stuff so that I can take a nap. In my disgustingly long hair.

(JEAN *starts off after him, but they're both stopped by* ANNA, *though her comment is made directly to* HESTER.)

ANNA. I wonder how you can lift the soup spoon to your mouth. With so much at stake. At these dinners, I mean.

(COLIN *hesitates – wants to be present now for any conversation between his mother and* ANNA.)

HESTER. You get used to it. We're an arm of the government, you might say. Georgetown. Dinners in Georgetown. Or we were. And will be again.

COLIN. The once and future king. Teddy will bring it all back. Challenge Carter, win the nomination. *Resurgit.* And Chandler with him. And you with Chandler.

HESTER. He's never taken this as seriously as he should have, I'll tell you, because he's incapable of anything like proper awe. Which I have tried to invest in him since he was a child.

COLIN. Awe.

HESTER. *(as she takes* ANNA*'s hand, leading her to the window:)* Over there. Joseph Alsop's house. You know Alsop?

ANNA. He was a great columnist.

HESTER. One night Jack Kennedy came to his house for dinner looking (all –)

COLIN. (Here's the story.)

HESTER. (– troubled.) He told you? We all knew something was up. The guests were Kay and Philip Graham, myself and Colin's father, and Isaiah Berlin. "Isaiah," Kennedy asked at dinner –

COLIN. "What have the Russians historically done when another country pushed their backs against the wall?"

HESTER. The next day we heard about the Cuban missile crisis. You see, he was secretly looking for advice, and he took it. That's the way it used to be. A president was able to get out of the White House, come to Georgetown, and learn something just because someone brilliant happened to be at dinner. Nixon did away with all that.

COLIN. Vietnam did away with all that.

HESTER. Fair enough. But Nixon killed it by deciding to be afraid of us, and now this band of mugwumps in the White House, this southern cabal –

COLIN. Spoken like a true Southerner.

HESTER. But it can all come back. Say what you will about the Kennedys. They know how to use us to move a social agenda forward. And that is what we are about. So if dinner is sometimes tense with purpose, you do get used to it.

ANNA. I very much hope to.

(Something in this stops HESTER, *if very briefly.)*

HESTER. Come, Colin, promise to be my good son tonight, and I'll help you clear out Chandler's things.

COLIN. *(as she's leading him off)* Just don't try and get anywhere near me with a pair of scissors.

(**HESTER** *and* **COLIN** *exit.*)

(*Left alone onstage,* **ANNA** *and* **JEAN** *smile tightly at one another.*)

ANNA. I'm very sorry about your husband. Colin has told me about it. You lost him in the Second World War?

JEAN. Oh, all that was so long ago. Forgotten, really.

ANNA. Not by everyone.

(**ANNA** *exits.*)

(**JEAN** *watches her go, then approaches the table, where her plate of toast has been left. She's hoping to find some toast remaining, but all that's left is crumbs. Still watching the place where* **ANNA** *has exited, she begins to gather the crumbs onto her thumb and then lifts her thumb to her mouth to lick them off, all that's left of her breakfast.*)

(*Lights down.*)

Scene Two

(That evening.)

(Blackout music: Frank Sinatra's "It's Nice to Go Travelling")

*(Lights up to reveal the living room in the aftermath of that evening's dinner. Candlelight, with some candles snuffed. Seated around a small table, **ANNA**, looking gorgeous in **HESTER**'s dress, and now wearing earrings. Also seated are **CHANDLER HARRIS**, a patrician liberal senator from Virginia, in his 50's, and **GEORGE MALLONEE**, the Senator from Kentucky, roughly **CHANDLER**'s age. They are all three smoking cigars, and holding snifters of brandy. Of the three, only **CHANDLER** looks like he's not having a very good time.)*

MALLONEE. I must say, Chandler, I'm admiring this young lady's balls.

*(**ANNA** laughs, coughs.)*

But you seem nervous.

CHANDLER. The last time a woman did this, refused to leave the gentlemen to their post-prandial drinks – I think it was Sally Quinn, before she got it, before she learned Washington.

*(**MALLONEE** refills **ANNA**'s brandy snifter.)*

MALLONEE. Young lady.

ANNA. Only if you do, Senator.

MALLONEE. I don't mind.

(He refills his own.)

Go on, Chandler.

CHANDLER. I'm just remembering how curtailed the conversation became. I believe we spent a long time pondering Adlai Stevenson's last recorded words.

ANNA. What were they?

CHANDLER. "I would like to sit in the shade with a glass of wine and watch the young people dance".

MALLONEE. That's the last thing he said? Good God, I hope it's not the last thing I say. I want to drop dead dancing. The young people can go to hell. Forgive me, young lady.

ANNA. I'll forgive you if you tell me what you usually do. The men alone. While the women go off. In this charmingly quaint fourteenth century ritual.

MALLONEE. We get naked and wrestle in the mud.

ANNA. Well, don't let me stop you.

MALLONEE. Chandler?

CHANDLER. Where do we find the mud, I wonder.

ANNA. Seriously. What do you do?

CHANDLER. We could tell you. But then we'd have to kill you.

 (**MALLONEE** *laughs.*)

MALLONEE. Tell her, for God's sake, Chandler.

CHANDLER. It's very dull. We use the bathroom. We tell an off-color story or two. We enjoy the privilege, in the understanding that it is soon to be taken away.

ANNA. Tell an off-color story. Please. I would love to hear one.

MALLONEE. Oh, you spoil all the pleasure. It's never –

CHANDLER. *(Seamlessly picking up the cue, as the two of them will continue to do with one another throughout this part of the scene.)* Deliberate. It's never a planned thing. It's something that happens.

MALLONEE. Exactly.

CHANDLER. Or funny, either. It's never really all that funny. Wouldn't you say?

MALLONEE. No. It's all about one guy leaning over another guy's shoulder, his hand on your shoulder, breathing close to you. Maybe you've been fighting all day about some pissant provision in some damn bill that can't move out of committee –

CHANDLER. Exactly.

MALLONEE. And suddenly he's a man. He's just a man with slightly foul breath. And the mere fact that he's using certain words –

CHANDLER. The great words. The great language.

MALLONEE. Dick. Tit. Ass.

CHANDLER. Shakespearean language.

MALLONEE. Suddenly he's familiar. He's not the asshole across the table holding up a bill because he won't agree to a little kickback to the bloc of farmers you've got to answer to.

CHANDLER. Screw the farmers, you almost say.

MALLONEE. I'll deal with farmers, you say. The bill moves a little closer to an agreed-upon state because the man you've spent the whole day –

CHANDLER. Fulminating against.

MALLONEE. He's just, goddammit, he's just a guy. You almost love him.

(*A beat.*)

ANNA. I could never penetrate that. Which is what makes me sad.

CHANDLER. Don't be sad. It's going. We might as well invite the others in. If I know Hester, she'll have had her ear to the door this whole time anyway.

(*He exits.*)

MALLONEE. Where'd your good looking boyfriend go?

ANNA. He seems to have picked up something weird on the plane.

MALLONEE. That's right. You're just back from England.

ANNA. Yes.

MALLONEE. Hate the place.

ANNA. Do you?

MALLONEE. Yes. Hate it. Don't tell anyone?

ANNA. Why?

MALLONEE. They don't like us. Don't like me, anyway. They pretend they do. But have you ever been with anybody who's smiling at you, but you can tell they can't wait for you to leave so they can make fun of you?

ANNA. Yes, I have.

MALLONEE. Then there's the goddamn history. So much of it. Westminster. Whitehall. Like a weight on your back. Great thing about this country is we don't have to have a history if we don't want one. We can be as selective as we like. Go on citing George Washington and the Constitution, those'll cover a man for just about anything.

(to ANNA's unspoken question)

I'm serious.

ANNA. I don't doubt your seriousness.

MALLONEE. Or my intelligence. Secret of politics. Keep things simple. Hark back all you can. People feel like the government is out to take away their freedoms, and goddammit, they don't like that. You've always got to make it look like you're on the side of giving something back. Ever been to Kentucky?

ANNA. Not yet.

(He looks at her with new interest. CHANDLER leads the women on, from where they have been waiting in an adjacent room – HESTER, now looking fully "staged", and CAROLYN MALLONEE. MRS. MALLONEE looks very much the Kentucky doyenne – at least the 70's version of it – but with a Lauren Bacall sangfroid. They are all in the midst of a conversation.)

HESTER. We've been discussing *Apocalypse Now*. And you –

CHANDLER. Don't be coy. You know exactly what we've been discussing.

MALLONEE. We saw that movie.

HESTER. Yes, and your wife was appalled by it.

CAROLYN. That's right. I was. Appalled.

MALLONEE. Oh, we both were. What was that?

CAROLYN. The whole movie, I was thinking, will someone please shave?

MALLONEE. Exactly. Like it was a goddamn rock and roll war.

HESTER. You're aware it's based on Joseph Conrad's *Heart of Darkness*.

(A beat.)

CAROLYN. You know, Mrs. Ferris, I almost resent that.

(As it slowly dawns on **HESTER** *that she's committed a faux pas:)*

My Congressional Ladies' Book Club is reading that novel right now. As we speak. "Mistah Kurtz, he dead."

(She lights a cigarette.)

HESTER. I stand corrected.

MALLONEE. Tell them what else you read.

CAROLYN. George.

MALLONEE. Tell them.

CAROLYN. *(She won't.)* I don't like showing off.

MALLONEE. Henry James.

HESTER. I stand so corrected.

MALLONEE. Called this town. Tell them. "The city of conversation". Got that one right.

HESTER. Why is it I haven't been invited into this book club?

CAROLYN. *(a velvet fist)* We started it, Congressional ladies from places like Kentucky and Iowa and Nebraska, to defend ourselves from people like you, Mrs. Ferris, who might think that because we come from backwater places, that we are backwater people.

HESTER. Do you know where I come from?

MALLONEE. It so happens I do. My staff does good work. Forrest City, Arkansas. Though you'd never know it.

CAROLYN. She's worked hard to lose her accent.

MALLONEE. Why would you want to do that?

HESTER. Have you ever been to Forrest City, Arkansas? Kentucky, on the other hand. A wonderful state.

We're such creatures of assumption. To think I would think that. A backwater person like myself. I've driven through Kentucky only twice, I'm sorry to say, and what I felt was how lush and beautiful it was.

CAROLYN. Flatterer.

MALLONEE. No. Let her. Go on.

HESTER. That – grass. And those wonderful white fences. Horses. I've felt this other places. Texas. Places no one up here thinks much about. But you drive through and you get a feeling, it comes over you, what it must be like to be from there, the pride you must feel. Which is not possible everywhere. Not, anyway, in Forrest City, Arkansas.

MALLONEE. *(having enjoyed* **HESTER** *'s little aria)* You've hit it. No one wants to leave.

HESTER. Which is why it seems silly to me that we should come to this city and feel we have to be able to quote Henry James, as if we all have to be all one thing. Something boiled down to an essence. When we're really so many things. We come from places we are so proud of, and want to protect, while at the same time understanding we are this odd and unwieldy but necessary union.

MALLONEE. Carolyn, She's absolutely right. I want you to quit that book club in the morning.

(He laughs loudly.)

*(***COLIN*** enters, having come from a long sojourn in the bathroom.)*

HESTER. Are you all right?

COLIN. *(holding his stomach gently)* Any – guess – as to how long that egg was in the refrigerator?

HESTER. The egg was fine. You drank too much, I think, at dinner.

COLIN. When you're tired, you do that.

MALLONEE. He's all right. Have some of this.

(He pours **COLIN** *brandy.)*

HESTER. I don't think so.

MALLONEE. Medicinal. Soothes the belly. An old Kentucky remedy.

(He winks at **HESTER.***)*

*(***COLIN** *takes the brandy, under his mother's disapproving stare.)*

And speaking of this odd and – what?

ANNA. "Unwieldy but necessary" –

MALLONEE. Union. You mind if we talk a smattering of business? I mean, I'd much rather talk about Henry James.

CAROLYN. George can't get enough of Henry James.

MALLONEE. Well, that's what these damn dinners are supposed to be about, aren't they? Chatter and culture and nuance, and we don't talk about the real thing.

CHANDLER. What's the real thing?

MALLONEE. Fact is, I'm having doubts about this bill.

(to the others:)

Excuse us, this is what we were supposed to be talking about when this charming young lady joined us for drinks after dinner.

CHANDLER. Doubts?

MALLONEE. A lesson in Washington. These young people might enjoy this. Teddy Kennedy is running for President.

HESTER. He hasn't quite announced yet.

MALLONEE. Teddy Kennedy is running for President. And though Senator Kennedy seems to expect to be anointed, there will be primaries. Hard fought. You don't unseat a sitting President without hard fought. Some of these primaries will be in the South. He can't just win in the North. He's got to beat Carter somewhere in the South. So the question becomes –

ANNA. Carter's a Southerner.

MALLONEE. So the black vote becomes crucial. Who wins the black vote. Teddy gets an idea. From his august position as chair of the Senate Judiciary Committee, make a dramatic statement. Remind people of what the Kennedys stand for. Federal judges can no longer belong to all-white country clubs.

CHANDLER. Sounds entirely reasonable to me.

MALLONEE. Of course it does. If reason was the whole ball of wax.

HESTER. Strom Thurmond has signed on.

MALLONEE. Strom Thurmond, having spent his entire working life putting down the Negro race in this country, can afford a valedictory gesture of munificence.

HESTER. Senator Mallonee, your backwoods manner masks a certain eloquence.

MALLONEE. Thank you.

CAROLYN. Watch her, George.

HESTER. You have nothing at all to fear.

MALLONEE. But a man like me. Not valedictory but still in the arena. In Kentucky. There are judges who might well look askance.

HESTER. Rise above them.

MALLONEE. No, that's exactly where you're wrong. Nice men. Good men. Reasonable and enlightened men who enjoy a mint julep on the veranda. And when the veranda happens to be at the Royal Oaks Country Club, closed since time immemorial to our black brethren, well, there are friends there on the veranda with them.

(pause)

Tell them to resign? To lose forever the sight of that magenta-colored Kentucky sun falling behind the oak trees?

HESTER. You can't be serious.

MALLONEE. I am.

HESTER. Well, then, open it up.

(to his silent, skeptical question:)

The club.

MALLONEE. Oh yes, and watch our black friends stream in. They can't wait to get into the Royal Oaks. This is all a farce, Mrs. Ferris. Those places are about tradition, that's all they are. What's a black man going to find to enjoy on that veranda? The food is terrible, the drinks are weak. But the people who want to be there have to feel they can still do things even if they know those things aren't perfect.

CHANDLER. Teddy will make a speech, just prior to the vote, calling you the last holdout and the biggest obstacle to racial progress since Bull Connor. You will then be free to stage a dramatic turnabout and vote yes, earning yourself a place in the revised, updated version of *Profiles in Courage*.

MALLONEE. It so happens I don't want him to make that speech. I do not want to endear myself to my constituents by being called a racist. It so happens I'm not, and they do not want to see me that way. Trust me on this. But I do not believe in denying a man his beloved – ingrained – unbad – freedoms just because an entitled candidate is looking for a straw issue with which to beat a sitting President.

(A beat. COLIN pours himself more brandy, suddenly nervous.)

HESTER. Colin.

ANNA. In Minneapolis, where I come from, Senator.

MALLONEE. Lovely place, Minneapolis. The falls. Majestic.

ANNA. Or not the city of Minneapolis, exactly, but a small town north of there, there's a feeling – you can sense it when you talk to anyone – that we've gone about as far as we need to. That – I think what people would most like from Washington is a bill declaring the 60's officially over.

HESTER. Is that how they think in Minneapolis? I've often wondered.

COLIN. Let her talk.

ANNA. And by "the 60's", what they mean is the stranglehold of the Northeast – of a worldview that insists we all need to be legislatively coerced into good behavior. That seven or eight highly educated people in New York and Washington know what's best for the rest of us.

HESTER. God save us from the wisdom of the small town.

MALLONEE. Go on.

ANNA. The Kennedys, for instance. The long, ambiguously positive rule of a very rich, highly suspect American family with a set of ideals forged in the crucible of the trust fund.

HESTER. Perhaps you don't read the polls, young lady.

ANNA. My name is Anna.

HESTER. Forgive me. Anna. If the election were being held today –

ANNA. It so happens it isn't. Being held today.

HESTER. Senator Mallonee reads polls. And understands, I'm sure, what life might be like under a new Democratic President who will not appreciate a signature bill being held back by a single vote.

MALLONEE. Oh, I can appreciate that very well.

ANNA. But who is to say that is going to happen, Senator. Another whole – possibility exists.

MALLONEE. (*an understanding growing between them*) So they tell me.

ANNA. There is a feeling – not yet reflected in the polls – that a suppressed energy is waiting to be released. People like my father might begin to have a voice.

MALLONEE. And your father is –

ANNA. A small city cop, who feels, quite rightly as it happens, that something in this country has been lost.

MALLONEE. It has. Indeed it has. Governor Reagan speaks to that, doesn't he? Quite well.

HESTER. God help us.

ANNA. Governor Reagan, or someone much like him – but let's say, for the purpose of argument, *him*, might restore people's simple belief that the old agreements, the ones that made this a great country – personal responsibility, neighborhood, family, a reassertion of people's basic freedoms – have to come back. Or we're quite possibly lost.

MALLONEE. I like what I'm hearing.

HESTER. Oh, don't we all. The old Jeffersonian vision. A country of yeomen farmers. Or cops, with all due respect. who conveniently forget that liberalism came along to take care not only of the poor and the disenfranchised blacks, but of the unions that gave your father what I expect has been a (comfortable life).

ANNA. (The Democrats took) us a certain distance. but now they've walked off the cliff and don't yet realize there's nothing under them.

HESTER. Be specific, please. I feel like I'm being taken back in a time capsule to Barry Goldwater's '64 campaign.

ANNA. All right then. Look where the winner of that election took us. Deeper into a war he refused to win. Into an enormous defeat that left us devastated as a country in terms of purpose. No one respects us in the world anymore.

HESTER. Does it interest you that your boyfriend – excuse me, fiancée – protested that war? Dragged his college buddies – a very messy, smelly crew, as I recall – into this house so that they had comfortable beds to sleep in after their protests –

ANNA. Exactly. The beds were always comfortable for the elite that protested that distasteful war. But an enormous – majority – those that slept in less comfortable beds – lost something in those protests.

MALLONEE. I always felt that.

ANNA. A belief in their ability to have a voice. A belief that their country still had the potential to be a force for good in the world. They were drowned out.

MALLONEE. Yes.

HESTER. Speaking of voices – Colin, do you have one?

COLIN. I do, as it happens.

CHANDLER. George, I think you and I might want to continue this in private – shall we take a little walk around the block?

MALLONEE. I'm enjoying this.

CHANDLER. I fear it's going to descend into a family washing its dirty laundry.

MALLONEE. The best kind of descent after a pleasant dinner party. Carolyn, do you have any objection to our staying?

CAROLYN. *(smiling pointedly at* **HESTER***)* None at all.

(A beat.)

HESTER. Colin.

COLIN. I always felt – something phony about it – me and my friends. Our dirty, expensive clothes. The celebrity studded marches. Robert Lowell and Norman Mailer at the barricades. Why did people hate us? Why did the construction workers want to beat us up? It was about being young and excited, but you never felt you were –

(difficult for him)

– an American.

HESTER. So at the London School of Economics, you met an example of that corn-fed breed.

(The next two lines should be spoken simultaneously, with **HESTER** *riding right over them.)*

CHANDLER. Hester.

ANNA. The contempt you feel.

HESTER. The sparkling star of the London School of Economics production of *State Fair*. I bet you looked wonderful in gingham and tight jeans. Did you appear with a hayseed between your teeth?

ANNA. The contempt for the vast majority in this country. Legislate anti-racism, so that people will actually hate the strait-jacket you've put them in, rather than allow the inevitable progress of decent people changing their attitudes over time –

HESTER. How much time do you think we have? You're asking black people, just wait. They've waited.

ANNA. It does them no real good when people are forced to think differently.

HESTER. No. I think it does. Senator Mallonee?

MALLONEE. Wonderful. She's right, of course. Let some new energy out. Forcing people –

HESTER. What is this "new energy"? Is it that washed up movie star governor? Is it him you're talking about?

ANNA. You can't see what he represents –

CHANDLER. Calm down, Hester.

ANNA. Because you're locked in the past.

HESTER. Am I, really? Tell me what's the difference between being locked in the past and insisting people remember it.

ANNA. Mrs. Ferris, I say this with respect. I know you see me – us – Governor Reagan – as barbarians at the gates. But you have lost touch. Do you have any idea how deep it is right now, people's desire to love their country again?

HESTER. Oh please.

ANNA. It's very hard to perceive that desire when you're locked inside this –

MALLONEE. City of conversation.

HESTER. So this is what I sent you to London for.

COLIN. You didn't send me.

CHANDLER. George, I hate to take us away from this cheerful scene, but we do need a little time together before tomorrow's meeting.

MALLONEE. *(He's been fascinated by the exchanges.)* Oh, yes. And it's getting late. Fascinating, though. Carolyn?

CAROLYN. George, I think you might ask this young woman to come and see you.

MALLONEE. *(picking up a little slowly on her hint)* What? Yes. Of course. Would you come see me? Call my office and come – I don't suppose I could entice you to come work for me?

ANNA. *(handling this masterfully)* I would very much like to come and see you.

MALLONEE. Call my office. Be sure you do. I'll alert my assistant. A stimulating evening, Mrs. Ferris. Do we have to go?

HESTER. Aren't you – wouldn't you be nervous, Mrs. Mallonee, having such an attractive young woman working with your husband?

CAROLYN. *(She smiles.)* Thank you for an illuminating evening. If you're really interested in our Ladies' Book Club, I'd be happy to put your name forward.

HESTER. Thank you. I'll consider it.

CHANDLER. I'll see you both out.

(**CHANDLER, MALLONEE** and **CAROLYN** *exit.*)

(tense silence)

ANNA. I'm going to – take off the dress. Leave it hanging somewhere. So you can take it to the cleaners.

(A beat.)

ANNA. I meant it. I have nothing but the highest respect for what your generation achieved. Standing up to the Russians. That was huge, and brave. Not to mention your sister's sacrifice.

(She exits, leaving **HESTER** *and* **COLIN** *alone.)*

HESTER. I didn't read the date on your letter wrong, did I?

COLIN. We found out about this dinner. Jean let it slip in her last letter. Anna thought it might be an opportunity. He was the right sort of Senator. It actually cost quite a bit to get the tickets changed.

(He tries to pour himself another drink.)

HESTER. Stop.

(A beat.)

Who are you now?

COLIN. I was contemplating my future in London. Like everyone else. From my gorgeous privileged position. I would come back with my advanced degree, and you would no doubt find me a job on someone's staff – Senator Church's. Senator Bayh's from Indiana. Senator Moynihan's. The right Senator. I would go to lunches in Washington. I would have dinners here. Date a tight blonde from the Wharton School of Business by way of Stanford. Liberal pedigree. You would groom me.

HESTER. Wretched. Yes. Terrible. Your mother's stranglehold.

COLIN. And it occurred to me. I would never know what it was to be –

HESTER. Oh please. If you say you want to be an "American" one more time I'll scream. We are all Americans.

COLIN. What it was to feel something for this country. I would only know what it was to be educated at Sidwell Friends and Harvard.

HESTER. So you met, in the form of a long-legged, untight blonde, the country itself.

COLIN. Dismiss it that way. I started to listen, that's all. To other voices.

HESTER. And what did they tell you, Colin? I listened to your girlfriend and I know what she wants. Is that what you believe now, Colin? Coming from this house, is that what you believe?

COLIN. I don't want to offer it up to you.

HESTER. You have fallen for something, Colin. You were always a boy who got good grades but did not think in complex ways. That's my assessment. It's always been my assessment.

COLIN. Do you have any idea what a squeeze that is. What a tight, deballing squeeze.

HESTER. Well, there it is. You go off to London, all the bright new ideas are about the decline of liberalism. Let's forget everything we learned in Vietnam. Let's just love our country again. Let's go out and be a force for good in the world. Let me get on that bus, my son says. All the cute girls are on that bus. The wind is blowing in that direction.

COLIN. Stop.

HESTER. And it allows me to be free of my mother, doesn't it?

COLIN. It would never occur to you that I could have a thought – a set of thoughts – outside of the bounds of Georgetown.

HESTER. Why should that occur to me?

(At the foot of the stairs, ANNA appears. A very different ANNA, her makeup gone, in pajamas. Her hair pulled up. Scrubbed. Almost innocent and virginal looking.)

ANNA. Colin. I just came to see if you were coming to bed.

COLIN. Yes. I'm coming. In a minute.

(He reaches for her hand.)

ANNA. We won't be staying here, Mrs. Ferris. We've made other arrangements. Just tonight, if that's all right. You won't have to put up with me after tonight.

COLIN. Just for the rest of my life.

ANNA. *(A beat.)* Yes. Just that.

(She goes.)

(HESTER stands. She and COLIN look at each other.)

(Lights down. End of Act One.)

ACT TWO

Scene One

(Mid-September, 1987.)

(In the dark: Teddy Kennedy's "Robert Bork's America" speech, denouncing the Supreme Court nominee. ["Robert Bork's America is a land in which women would be forced into back alley abortions, blacks would sit at segregated lunch counters, rogue police could break down citizens' doors in midnight raids, schoolchildren could not be taught about evolution, writers and artists would be censored at the whim of the government."])

(Lights come up to reveal the living room only superficially changed, the same furniture with some new slipcovers, perhaps more memorabilia on the credenza. The only really new thing is a TV with a VCR attached [the screen turned away from us], and a stack of children's videos on top of it. A child's toys mildly clutter the space.)

(A ball comes bouncing on from the kitchen area, followed by ETHAN, the six year old son of COLIN and ANNA. ETHAN chases the ball onstage while HESTER, behind him, talks into a cordless phone while holding a piece of paper in her hands. The eight years that have passed since the time of Act One should not have caused huge physical changes in her, though she's in her late fifties now. She wears glasses.)

HESTER. Ethan, be careful. The ball is not to be thrown inside.

(into the phone:)

39

HESTER. *(cont.)* Ralph, I'm sorry. It's my grandson trying to destroy some perfectly good if faded old furniture.

(She puts the piece of paper down, holds out her hand to **ETHAN** *for the ball, trying to do two things at once.)*

Okay. The wording should be this.

(to **ETHAN***'s refusal to hand over the ball:)*

Ethan. Give it to me.

(back into the phone, picking up the piece of paper:)

No. No, Ralph. It should read "The Reagan administration has fired a parting shot of contempt for the rights of minorities and women in the nomination to the Supreme Court of Robert Bork".

(Toward the end of this statement, **JEAN** *enters.)*

Too many words?

JEAN. Ethan, come.

ETHAN. Don't want to.

JEAN. Young man, I don't believe I'm giving you a choice.

(As **HESTER** *continues her phone conversation, there should be another conversation, in dumbshow, in which* **HESTER** *tells* **JEAN** *it's okay to leave the boy alone, while she wrestles the ball away from him. Their relationship is playful;* **ETHAN** *does not make her work physically hard to wrest the ball away.)*

HESTER. *(into the phone)* All right. Yes. We'll simplify the beginning.

(reading:)

"Robert Bork thought it was just fine that an American company give women the choice of being sterilized or losing their jobs. He could find no constitutional basis for desegregating schools in Washington, D.C." This is all about pointing out how narrow his vision of the Law is. And then urge people to call Senator Heflin. Heflin is huge, Ralph. He's the vote we need on Judiciary.

(It's at this point that she should have wrested the ball away.)

All right, I have Ethan till four, Ralph, and then I'll come over. Yes, we'll type it up. But remember, it is not to be known that I'm doing this. I am doing this unofficially, Ralph.

(She shuts the phone off in triumph.)

JEAN. I don't see how you can become involved with this and still watch a six year old boy.

HESTER. Oh stop. I've done it all my life. We need to type this up and bring it over.

ETHAN. Throw me the ball.

HESTER. I cannot throw you the ball inside, Ethan.

(She points to the array of photographs she keeps on the credenza:)

These may look like silly things to you , but they are great men who have changed the world, and if you were wise, you would study them.

*(**ETHAN** smiles at her, as if to let her know how silly that notion is.)*

Come here.

ETHAN. No.

HESTER. Come here, come here. Let me smell this hair.

(She draws him toward her. He allows it.)

This is the most delicious hair. Jean, have you smelled this hair?

JEAN. I have not. I don't go around smelling small boys' hair.

HESTER. We are going to keep this evil man from going to the Supreme Court, Ethan. This man who wants to turn back the tide of the last fifty years, to keep black people and women from progressing.

*(**ETHAN** picks his nose.)*

Ethan.

JEAN. Hester, you would do well to remember he may be getting a different message from his parents. And you've made a promise to Colin. Be careful.

HESTER. I'm sorry. Of course. You didn't hear anything bad about this man from me, did you, Ethan?

ETHAN. Yes. I did.

HESTER. I can't help it. After seven years of Reagan and all these awful people running things, I feel like Scrooge waking up from his visit with the third ghost – which one is it?

ETHAN. The Ghost of Christmas Yet to Come.

HESTER. Exactly. He is so smart, Jean. The Yet to Come is all going to be different now.

JEAN. *(She is by the TV, gesturing to the pile of videos.)* Ethan, why don't you come here and pick out a video while your grandmother and I type up this letter.

(He does so.)

Cinderella.

HESTER. Very good choice. A young feminist already. Now. Show us how to use it.

Put on your glasses, Jean. We should know this.

(They watch him expertly put in the video and turn it on, with the use of a remote device.)

God, he's like Thomas Edison. I will never in a million years know how to do this.

ETHAN. It's easy. You push this.

HESTER. Yes, but you see at a certain point, Ethan, it's easier to defeat a Supreme Court nominee than it is to learn new technology. Now will you sit quietly and watch this until we've finished typing this up?

*(***ETHAN*** settles himself, as the movie comes on.)*

JEAN. Oh dear, it's not at the beginning.

ETHAN. It's all right. I don't like the beginning.

*(***HESTER*** and ***JEAN*** have every intention of leaving, but from the moment they start watching Cinderella, they can't tear themselves away.)*

HESTER. *(to* JEAN*'s prompt that they leave:)* Yes, just one second.

(They watch, intrigued.)

JEAN. It's really very anti-cat, isn't it? I never realized that.

HESTER. Oh, entirely favors the dog. Not so good about women, either. Ethan, maybe there's another movie.

ETHAN. I like the Grand Duke.

HESTER. He likes the Grand Duke. Very well. Just don't pay any attention to the relations between women, all right? The stepsisters. It's very false. Women don't treat each other that way.

*(*JEAN *looks meaningfully at* HESTER, *who doesn't notice.)*

We've only got a little to do now. We'll be back.

(As they leave, HESTER *turns back once, to look at the boy.)*

JEAN. Hester.

HESTER. Was Colin that beautiful, Jean?

JEAN. He looked exactly like him.

HESTER. I don't remember. Why don't I remember? Why does it all seem a blur?

*(*JEAN *leads* HESTER *out. As they disappear:)*

Was Colin that smart, Jean?

(Alone, ETHAN, *watching the video, begins picking his nose; after a moment,* ETHAN *reaches inside the drawer where* HESTER *has hidden the ball. He tosses it. It takes a couple of bounces and is caught, on his entrance, by* CHANDLER, *who enters carrying an overstuffed briefcase. The move required to catch the ball strains* CHANDLER. ETHAN, *observant, takes this in. Of all of them, it's* CHANDLER *who's most changed by the last eight years, most of which he has spent in the unaccustomed position of being a member of the minority party. He looks worn out by long effort.)*

CHANDLER. I don't think your grandmother wants you to play fast and loose with this, young man. Have they left you alone?

(*ETHAN doesn't answer. He's a bit intimidated by* **CHANDLER**.)

Hester! I'm out of the hearings! Hester!

HESTER. *(offstage)* Yes! Be right with you.

CHANDLER. Is there something to drink, do you suppose, Ethan?

(*He goes to where the drinks are kept, pours himself a drink.*)

(*noting that the TV is on:*)

Cinderella, is it? Boys like you shouldn't be inside on a day like this.

(*ETHAN doesn't answer.*)

Tell you what, since you're so intent on throwing this ball around, why don't we go outside and have a proper catch? What do you say to that?

ETHAN. Won't it hurt you?

(*HESTER enters, her glasses on, carrying an overstuffed folder.*)

HESTER. How did it go?

CHANDLER. Well, I think. Heflin went on a diatribe against Bork's beard.

HESTER. Is that good?

CHANDLER. Very good, I'd say. A signal, perhaps, as to which way he's leaning. The Senator from Alabama cannot convince his home base that the Judge should be rejected simply for his racist rulings, but what he can do is convince them he's undeserving because of his general weirdness. The beard, which, I will grant you, is very weird. And the agnosticism, which to 99 percent of the country reads as atheism.

HESTER. I can't believe it's going so well.

CHANDLER. I'm trying to entice this young man into a game of catch, outside. I caught him red-handed.

HESTER. Throwing the ball? I should be mad if I weren't so ecstatic. Jean is upstairs typing a letter I've drafted to run in newspapers in Alabama. And I've got to find the date of that article Bork wrote saying that white business owners had no obligation to serve blacks.

(She is poring through her folder, looking for the article.)

CHANDLER. *(He goes for a refill of his drink.)* It was 1963.

HESTER. You're sure?

CHANDLER. *(nods, confident of his facts)* '63.

(HESTER looks at him, grateful, then goes to the stairs to call up to JEAN.)

HESTER. Jean! It was 1963!

JEAN. All right.

HESTER. *(back to CHANDLER)* Thank you.

(She finds a place to stash the folder.)

CHANDLER. Any chance in the world I could get you to sit on my lap?

HESTER. Chandler.

CHANDLER. A moment's relief.

HESTER. Do you know what happened this morning in Montgomery, Alabama?

CHANDLER. I do, in fact. Seventeen separate groups – blacks, women, labor – held hands at a press conference, begging the Senate to reject the nomination of Robert Bork. Now quit focusing on the South. The real enemy is those overgrown boys from the Reagan freshman class – those pipsqueaks elected seven years ago on Reagan's coattails who have somehow managed to hang on – though they all look like – who was he? – the little boy on *The Andy Griffith Show?*

ETHAN. Opie.

CHANDLER. Opie. Exactly. they all manage to look exactly like Opie would look after attending a boot camp for draconian Republicans. According to those wet behind the ears back benchers, it's not blacks and women who need to be protected. It's fetuses. It's white Italian boys being denied places on their hometown fire departments because a black man has taken his place, courtesy of Affirmative Action. What we really need is the fetuses and the Italian boys to hold hands at a press conference and declare that they no longer need protection, thank you very much, Judge Bork.

(On the end of this, **CHANDLER** *has refilled his drink.)*

HESTER. That's your third, I think.

CHANDLER. Is it? Who's counting? Is someone counting? I wonder why. Besides, look at me.

(as he glances at himself in the mirror:)

I'm a wreck. And that's after a good day. I used to be handsome, didn't I?

ETHAN. *(turns away from Cinderella)* I don't like this part.

CHANDLER. Ethan, why don't you wait outside and – better yet, do you have a hardball and a mitt?

HESTER. He loves this ball.

CHANDLER. *(harder)* All right then, Ethan. Wait in the yard, will you, and we'll throw this rather silly ball around.

*(***ETHAN***, a little frightened now of* **CHANDLER**, *takes the ball.)*

HESTER. Just a little while, Ethan. You can watch *Cinderella* later.

*(***ETHAN*** *runs out.)*

Don't be sharp with him. You frighten him.

CHANDLER. Boys need to be a little frightened, Hester. You treat him too delicately.

HESTER. The gate. I need to be sure the gate is locked.

(She exits. Alone, **CHANDLER** *stand at the window, drinking.* **JEAN** *comes in, with the typed sheet of paper.)*

JEAN. You look tired, Chandler.

CHANDLER. Long day. Join me in one.

JEAN. You know I can't. Too much to do.

CHANDLER. She has you hopping. Does she never give you a break?

JEAN. *(a bit of pique)* Chandler, you know I've been working on this just as long as Hester has. It's my work, too.

CHANDLER. *(backing off, but still jocular)* All right, all right.

JEAN. *(giving in, but not without noting his mild condescension)* The hearings went well?

CHANDLER. Smashing.

(HESTER enters, a bit breathless.)

HESTER. It was locked.

JEAN. *(on her way out)* I left you the typescript.

HESTER. Keep an eye on Ethan, would you, Jean? Just for a minute?

(JEAN exits. HESTER immediately takes up the typescript, begins checking it.)

Where were we? Chandler, I have to take this to Ralph Neas as soon as Colin gets here to pick up Ethan.

CHANDLER. You know precisely where we were. We were speaking about a lap. We were speaking about an old man who needs sexual reassurance.

HESTER. Does he? I wouldn't have thought so.

CHANDLER. *(as he approaches her and she eludes him)* Why are you so skittish?

HESTER. I feel like if I give in to anything all this is all going to fall apart – and we're so close, Chandler. We're so close to our first real victory in seven years.

CHANDLER. *(He grabs HESTER and draws her to him so that she lands in his lap.)* Yes, but while we are wresting power back, can we for five minutes forget the blacks and the women –

(COLIN enters, unseen, as CHANDLER is unbuttoning HESTER's shirt.)

CHANDLER. – and the fetuses.

(in reaction to her breasts:)

Oh nice. And the poor Italian boys shut out of F.D. 104.

HESTER. Stop.

CHANDLER. I will not.

(COLIN clears his throat. He, too, holds a briefcase. This older COLIN has a moustache.)

HESTER. Colin. This old goat has been distracting me.

CHANDLER. She's correct. I'm an old goat. There's no excuse for me. I see we all broke early today.

COLIN. Yes. Who's watching him?

HESTER. He's out in the yard, waiting for Chandler, who promised him a game of catch.

(COLIN looks out the window.)

I checked the gate. He's safe. Jean's keeping an eye.

COLIN. Is this how it usually goes?

HESTER. You know it doesn't. Now stop it, Colin. You're early. Don't be prudish.

CHANDLER. Your son was watching *Cinderella* while your mother was typing a letter for (Ralph) –

HESTER. *(overlapping with some urgency)* (Just) a letter.

CHANDLER. I promised him a catch and I don't intend to disappoint him. It will do me good. You can join us, you know. though God forbid some photographer from the Post catches us. The two sides playing catch together? Is bipartisanship returning to the Capitol?

COLIN. *(as CHANDLER makes his way out)* Thanks, I might join you.

HESTER. Be careful, Chandler. You've been drinking. Go easy on him.

(CHANDLER has exited. HESTER and COLIN alone.)

HESTER. I'm sorry you walked in on that.

COLIN. Oh, come on. I'm not really a prude. You deserve a sex life, don't you?

(Maybe he adjusts her dress. There's still an affection between them.)

HESTER. I take it you boys are playing rough with one another in committee.

COLIN. It's a big fight, isn't it? Huge. Defining. The old man's legacy.

HESTER. Is that what you all call Reagan now? "The old man"?

COLIN. *(deflecting her jibe)* How was he today? Ethan.

HESTER. Wonderful. He's always wonderful.

COLIN. *(watching the game of catch out the window)* Look at that. He can throw, can't he? I taught him that.

(catching himself in a moment of self-soothing)

We're not going to lose, right? I mean, people will come to their senses on this one. A President gets to pick his Supreme Court.

(No answer from HESTER.*)*

You're not saying anything. You wouldn't be trying to undercut me on this one, would you? I mean, you're staying out. You promised me.

HESTER. Just don't expect me to keep my mouth shut. Approving the sterilization of women is not a subject that makes me want to take up my knitting and retire.

COLIN. *(His tiredness makes him more annoyed by this than he might otherwise be.)* He didn't approve the sterilization of women. He read the law. That company was within its rights. The man's not a radical.

HESTER. No. Sterilization's very mainstream.

COLIN. You know we can't talk about this.

HESTER. Let's not.

COLIN. Just what you promised. Be loyal to me. I don't care what you say in your little parties –

HESTER. Yes, I'll confine my passion to my little parties.

COLIN. It would be a huge embarrassment to me if my own mother were seen to be working against me.

(*A beat.*)

Oh, and by the way, I walked in early, I heard a bit of your love chat. Putting down fetuses, that's the way to build up your majority.

HESTER. He wants a little relief.

COLIN. Which any man deserves. Just, mother, some political advice. Fetuses are not going to go away. Just so you know that. People talk about emerging minorities, fetuses are actually the big emerging minority.

HESTER. Nice to be getting political advice from you. You're so much closer to the center.

COLIN. Stop.

HESTER. Colin.

COLIN. Yes?

(*She goes to him, wets her finger, smoothes his moustache.*)

HESTER. If you're going to have one of these, you need to take care of it. Trim it.

COLIN. Yes. Thank you. You don't like it.

HESTER. I didn't say that.

COLIN. You don't need to.

HESTER. It's very – Republican.

(*A moment between them, perhaps a pull back to their shared past, which* **COLIN** *resists.*)

COLIN. I'm going to join them outside. You mind?

HESTER. No. Of course not.

(*They look at each other a moment, held by something.*)

COLIN. I'm going outside.

(*He exits through the kitchen.* **HESTER** *looks out the window, watching long enough to give time for* **COLIN** *to join the game.* **JEAN** *enters, watches* **HESTER** *watching.*)

JEAN. Have you had a chance to look it over?

HESTER. No. I will. I just –

JEAN. You may want to hide that letter, Hester. While Colin is here.

HESTER. Oh God, yes.

(She removes the letter to a more hidden spot, inside a drawer.)

JEAN. Something the matter?

HESTER. Am I going too much against him?

JEAN. It's up to you, Hester.

(HESTER goes back to the window to watch. A beat.)

JEAN. Let me know if there are any corrections.

(ANNA enters. It's a different ANNA. She wears a suit. She's very official Washington. Her long hair is in a French twist. She carries a briefcase, stuffed even more than CHANDLER's was. She looks like she's rushed to get here.)

ANNA. I'm sorry. Everyone broke early today. I thought for once I could get here before Colin – did I beat him?

HESTER. He's outside, playing catch with Ethan and Chandler.

ANNA. Fuck. Sorry. How early did he leave?

JEAN. I'll tell them you're here.

ANNA. No, that's all right. They barely get a chance to do this, we're all so busy.

(She drops her briefcase.)

HESTER. Would you like something? I could have Jean make coffee.

ANNA. Oh, please, no more coffee. We live on coffee. We forget to have lunch sometimes. And I know better than to ask you for something to eat. Is it okay if I sit?

HESTER. Of course. You're tired.

JEAN. I'll leave you.

ANNA. Jean, you don't have to leave. I'm not going to insult anyone. Or be unpleasant. I'm just glad to have a moment to collapse.

JEAN. No. I have some things to do.

ANNA. Of course.

(JEAN *leaves. Awkward moment.* ANNA *and* HESTER *are not often alone.*)

So. What's the report? Ethan.

HESTER. He watched a little *Cinderella*.

ANNA. Is it good? It's been so long I don't remember. We try to do family nights – videos and such – I fall asleep. I had no idea how exhausting the prospect of defeat could be. That's something you must know a great deal about.

HESTER. I thought we weren't going to be insulting today.

ANNA. Is that an insult? Have our skins grown so thin?

(*Half-laughing. The moment is not a heavy one for her.*)

Hester.

(*A beat.*)

The thing is, we were riding so high this summer with Ollie North. Everyone expected your side would get us on that one. But then this handsome young soldier stands up and makes patriotism look sexy and the nation goes gaga. That was kind of thrilling. A nationwide school girl crush. Even the men.

HESTER. You're surprised by that?

ANNA. Men getting crushes on men? I wouldn't hear things like that. At Justice, everyone's so straight. You get to miss gay people, their jokes.

HESTER. Maybe you should visit the Republican side of the Senate more often.

ANNA. That's an old one of yours, isn't it? That kind of inside Washington joke. Republicans are all really gay. Ha ha. They're not, as a matter of fact. Because a man believes certain things doesn't necessarily mean he's repressing others.

HESTER. Your judge – the judge you have, I'm afraid, staked your career on – doesn't believe homosexuals have any rights under the Constitution.

ANNA. Yes. What an oversight on the part of the Founding Fathers not to have anticipated Christopher Street.

(A beat.)

I'm sorry. We're falling into a trap, aren't we? I really don't want to argue Judge Bork's virtues right now, with you. And though I'm perhaps making a mistake by revealing my slight fear that this one could be lost, I don't really believe that. We're going to win.

HESTER. Good. Let's talk about something else then, shall we? Would you like a drink?

(HESTER starts to move toward the drinks table.)

ANNA. Oh God, I'd have to say no. I mean, would that be the essence of bad mothering – I have fifteen extra minutes to spend with my child, I spend it drinking.

(as HESTER moves away from the drinks table:)

Yes, please.

HESTER. Scotch all right?

(ANNA nods, and HESTER pours and hands her a drink.)

It's not bad mothering to need a break now and then.

ANNA. *(after her first sip)* You're very good with him. With Ethan. I want you to know how much I appreciate that. It's usually Colin who comes, so I don't see, but I'm told, and maybe I do see the results. He talks about you.

HESTER. Thank you for saying that.

ANNA. You know, I make my little jokes, but I actually don't think I'm very good at it. Motherhood. I'm not a natural.

(A beat.)

Aren't you going to reassure me?

HESTER. I don't know what you do as a mother. I don't see enough.

ANNA. Fine. I'm only saying this because I thought you might offer something – support, or empathy, because I think maybe you were bad at it, too. Too busy, too close to power.

(to **HESTER**'s brittle but silent response:)

Colin wants a lot. Maybe he wants what you never gave him enough of. I don't know how Psychology works. I know how the Justice Department works. But with a child, you have these questioning little moments, don't you? This little boy. I expect things will just go along. He'll be six, eight. He'll go to school. The teachers will be nice. He'll throw a ball and be athletic. I'll marvel at him. My handsome, perfect son. Then it occurs to me that even if all of those things happen, he's still waiting for something from me. And what is that?

(A beat.)

I'm sorry. Maybe you could tell Senator Harris to cut this game short.

HESTER. Are you all right?

ANNA. No, actually. I hate that this fight over Bork is even happening. And I don't really want to talk about motherhood. I expected all of this would be a lot easier. I thought we would just rise and rise and change the country and people would be grateful. But they're not. They get used to what you've given them and begin to have scruples they never had when they were just hungry. We're still going to win, I don't doubt that. It's just that it's gotten harder and harder and it exhausts me.

HESTER. You live long enough, you come to understand that politics is about tides.

ANNA. Don't give me your truisms, please. You've got to stop talking to my little boy about Judge Bork.

(A beat.)

HESTER. I'm sorry. I had no idea.

ANNA. He comes home and he asks me questions. Why is the Judge bad? Grandma says he's bad. And I am tired and I don't know how to answer.

HESTER. Perhaps because he is. Bad.

ANNA. *(smiles)* He's my little boy.

HESTER. No one's taking him away from you.

ANNA. No? How much better, I think sometimes, if he was seeing some neutral day care worker in the afternoon. Someone drab and kind, so that when he came home and looked at me, he would see female brightness and that would be the most glowing moment in his day.

HESTER. Is this competitive?

(A beat.)

I hadn't realized I was hurting you in this way. I will promise not to say anything about Judge Bork in his presence – if I can help it.

ANNA. And the next one? After this one is over? Should we lose. Which we won't. But given the wild improbability, what about the next one? What about him?

HESTER. Or her.

(ANNA nods: not likely.)

You know, one of the nice things, I always believed, about Georgetown, was the way we all used to lay down our arms at the end of the day and become convivial. As if to say, though the battles are very real, we are all finally people, and we have to rest and break bread together in order to get up the next day and do battle again.

ANNA. Oh yes, the Georgetown rules. I think that would be a lot easier for me if I didn't find your side so repulsive. The tortoise shell glasses. The grooming of the liberal intelligentsia. The pinhead look. I like a sexy man. I like rough Republicans. I like drinking with them and I like their fuck you attitude and the fact that they come from places like I come from and played sandlot

baseball and worked after school. I understand them,
and when they pour me a drink it's filled to the brim
and they look at my ass and don't apologize –

HESTER. And tell me, what are you going to do with a son
who's none of those things?

ANNA. Ethan is still being (formed).

HESTER. (Send) him out to the sandlot, are you? Going to
get him a job stacking newspapers and ask him to turn
over part of his allowance for the rent on Connecticut
Avenue? Grow up.

ANNA. I think I'm going to ask Senator Harris to desist.

HESTER. Yes, that's the way they talk, isn't it, those rough,
sexy Republicans you like so much. "Desist." That's
the kind of word they use. Do you want to know
something? I have been waiting eight years to know
you, and I haven't made the first step. My son's wife,
people say, what's she like? I don't know how to answer.
I think, actually, she's false. She wants to be something
she's far too sophisticated to be.

ANNA. Stop.

HESTER. No. Why should I? We come here, we are changed
by this place. Face that. We become – a class. We have
to talk to one another, we have to come to terms. You
refuse. Don't keep thinking you're the fresh-faced
outsider from some backwater town in Minnesota.
You're like me now. You're a creature of this place.

(ETHAN comes running on.)

ETHAN. Grandma!

(with somewhat less enthusiasm:)

Mommy.

ANNA. I came early, Ethan. I thought we'd have the
afternoon together. A little of the afternoon.

(In reaction, ETHAN can't help looking at her briefcase.)

(CHANDLER comes on, followed by COLIN.)

CHANDLER. He had us sweating.

(seeing her)

Anna.

ANNA. Senator.

COLIN. What are you doing here?

ANNA. We all broke early. Is it a crime? I thought Ethan and I could do something.

COLIN. I thought I'd cook.

ANNA. Fine.

COLIN. Instead of take-out.

ANNA. Wonderful. But there's no problem with take-out.

COLIN. She hates my cooking.

ANNA. I thought we could go to that playground, Ethan.

COLIN. We could go together.

ANNA. How would you cook then?

COLIN. *(A beat.)* I wouldn't. We'd do take-out.

CHANDLER. I'll let this major debate go on in my absence. I need a shower. A pleasure, young man. Anna.

ANNA. Senator.

CHANDLER. Colin.

ANNA. Congratulations on a good day. Just don't count on too many more.

CHANDLER. We will see about that, won't we?

(He exits.)

COLIN. Come on, Ethan, let's get into your jacket.

ETHAN. I want to finish watching *Cinderella*.

ANNA. We can finish watching it at home, Ethan.

ETHAN. We don't have it at home.

ANNA. We don't?

HESTER. You can borrow this copy, Ethan.

ANNA. Thank you.

HESTER. The case is in that drawer.

(As soon as she says it, **HESTER** *realizes she's made a mistake. The case is in the same drawer where she hid the letter. Opening it,* **ANNA** *can see the letter in plain sight.)*

HESTER. *(cont.)* And we'll put the ball away in there, too.

(She tries to divert **ANNA***'s attention by putting the ball in the drawer, and then closing it, but it's too late.)*

Here you are.

(handing **ETHAN** *the case)*

*(***ANNA** *opens the drawer again, takes out the letter and begins reading it.)*

COLIN. Come on, let's go.

ETHAN. Why are you both here?

COLIN. The hearings on the judge ended early.

ETHAN. The judge is evil.

(A beat. **ANNA** *looks up from reading the letter.)*

COLIN. Ethan.

(He smiles testily, looks at **HESTER.** *)*

Have you – you're bad.

HESTER. I never.

COLIN. You did. You're bad.

HESTER. All right. I'm bad.

COLIN. *(trying to minimize his very real annoyance with his mother)* You make my job harder. You know that?

HESTER. I know that.

COLIN. Then don't. All right? A promise. Or are your promises not good?

All right, Ethan, I will give you a little lecture on why your blinkered grandmother is wrong on this one. She's frustrated because she can't do anything about the Judge. Come on, let's go. Anna?

ANNA. Umm. No. I'm staying a minute.

(to his confusion:)

ANNA. Just a minute. I'll meet you at that playground.

HESTER. Give Grandma a kiss.

(ETHAN *does.*)

COLIN. At the playground.

(COLIN *and* ETHAN *exit.*)

ANNA. What's this?

HESTER. It's the draft of a letter we're running in newspapers.

ANNA. "We"?

HESTER. I'm doing some very minor work with Ralph Neas. The Leadership Conference on (Civil Rights).

ANNA. (I'm familiar) with the organization. Does Colin know?

HESTER. No.

ANNA. *(reading from the letter)* "A parting shot." We're parting, is that the notion? The Republicans are parting? "Call Senator Heflin and express your opposition to Judge Bork." Where's this going?

HESTER. Newspapers in Alabama.

ANNA. Don't do this.

HESTER. It's not me alone. This is simply the wording.

ANNA. Hold it back. We need Heflin. He's leaning your way, but he's still undecided. He doesn't need more pressure. Hold it back.

HESTER. Why would I do that?

ANNA. Because if I tell Colin you did this – if I tell your son you lied to him, that you have been working in secret – you will lose him.

HESTER. How altruistic of you. Saving me from losing my son.

ANNA. It doesn't matter to you.

HESTER. Of course it does. But relations between a mother and son don't end over politics.

ANNA. Of course they do. Of course they do. This is a real fight, Hester. It's about who gets to shape the future. It matters.

HESTER. It's because it matters that I'm doing it. And afterwards, we will forgive.

ANNA. God, it must have been wonderful. The feast of civility that was old Washington. Hester, the stakes have changed. We are in this because we want fiercely to protect people.

HESTER. Fetuses and firemen.

ANNA. People you believe do not need protection, and we will not stop or temper the fight just to get along. Colin will not forgive you and neither will I.

HESTER. I think I can live with one of those options.

(A beat.)

Do you love him?

ANNA. Oh, truth or dare. Turning the tables. Do I love him?

HESTER. I watched your interchange before.

ANNA. And saw?

HESTER. Disrespect.

(A beat.)

Death to a marriage. Disrespect.

ANNA. You should know.

HESTER. Precisely. But he's my son.

ANNA. Who you're willing to lie to. Is that respect?

HESTER. Do you love him?

ANNA *(A beat.)* I'm worried about what this will do to us. Is doing. This fight. The prospect of defeat terrifies me because, you see, I think I will be all right, I have guts and I'm ruthless and I'm at Justice, and I will ultimately – find a way to stay in a good place. But Colin –

(A beat.)

Well, Colin works for Senator Gordon Humphrey of New Hampshire, and Gordon Humphrey, should this one go down, may become disgusted and choose not to run again – it's beginning to look that way – and then what is Colin but a man with a resume.

A nice man.

A nice man with a moustache.

(A beat.)

You know what I'm talking about. You marry a man, you marry his bright ambition, his spark, and then you watch, because you can't know, can you, watching a man's life is like watching a movie, a good movie, it's not quite predictable. Who will he turn out to be? Will the ambition lead him to something real, something great, or will it flatten out? He likes to cook.

HESTER. Crucify him.

ANNA. No, it's just – he's looking for ways to live the life lesser men want to live these days. The playground life. The domestic life. Nothing wrong with that except it's not what I'd hoped he'd turn into. Colin needs a victory. His Senator needs a victory to keep him in the game, and I am hoping that's enough to bring back Colin's spark.

So – tear this up, please. Don't be a part of a defeat that will be very hard for your son.

HESTER. You will stoop that low, will you? To pretend to have feelings for my son you clearly don't have just to secure a victory. If you love a man you don't give a damn about his ambition. Colin has always been – limited. Handsome. Bright. Athletic. But without brilliance. You married him knowing that. But now, what, the sex is not quite what it was? Is one of those ass-pinching Republicans over at Justice waiting to take his place? Don't make Bork's win or loss the fulcrum of your marriage. This is all about you. You don't want to lose.

ANNA. Of course I don't. And I don't have to. There's a philosophy out there that says it's good to lose sometimes, it seasons you. I say bullshit. I say win all the time. Become arrogant. Arrogance gives you

confidence and it's confidence that gives you bold
ideas and bold ideas are what move the world.

HESTER. *(shaking her head)* It makes no difference. Ralph
will just reword this and run it anyway.

ANNA. But if this letter does the trick, if Heflin's
switchboard is flooded with anti-Bork calls and that
pushes him over, I couldn't bear knowing it was you
behind it. I could not face you. I could not have my
little boy coming here.

HESTER. Oh. A threat.

ANNA. Yes. Tear it up or you don't see him again.

HESTER. I am the best thing in his life.

ANNA. *(A beat.)* I take back my argument about arrogance.
The best thing in his life? Do you believe that?

HESTER. If he has a mother who's willing to trade him for
a vote, I'd say yes. Yes I am the best thing in his life.
Ethan needs me.

ANNA. There is day care – good day care – all over
Washington.

HESTER. They will not care about him the way I do.

ANNA. Of course they won't.

HESTER. This is your son.

ANNA. Precisely.

HESTER. You'd do that.

ANNA. You have won your battles, Hester. Women, blacks,
they have won. I have sacrificed a measure of my
influence over my son out of respect for you. I know
what he's getting here – the liberal indoctrination –
but believe it or not, I have respected you enough to
allow that. But you will not leave it at that, will you?
You will not just be a grandmother and let history
move on.

HESTER. You'd like to turn us all out to pasture. But if no
one with a memory fights, then something else rushes
in to fill the vacuum. Your Great Communicator has
put this country up for sale, and the money boys are

salivating. But that's not enough. Now what they want is a judge ruling from the bench willing to use perfect heartless logic to rip down all the safeguards we have fought to put in place. I don't think you could even recognize that degree of heartlessness, never having quite located that muscle in your body. Women are doing fine, blacks are doing fine. Great, so let's move on. Let's help the rich. Let's help white men. Why not? They're so fun, they make such good jokes and they're such good ass-pinchers. I could not stay out of this! I could not stay out, and respect myself. You will bring this country down out of smug ignorance.

ANNA. *(Having to take a moment. She gathers her briefcase, seems about to leave.)* Bring the country down. We're trying to "bring it down." Only what you know can be good. Isn't that the logic? To protect the unborn, that's not good – no, because Georgetown didn't think of it. That certain white men might be hurting, that's not good, because it's such an old fashioned retrograde idea. Plow a whole group of people under because they don't fit into your chic, stylish world. They are hurting, Hester, but you are stuck and you can never see that.

HESTER. Oh, are you going to cry?

(COLIN enters, with ETHAN, in a hurry.)

COLIN. We forgot his project for tomorrow. He just told me about it. Where is it, Ethan?

(ETHAN is about to lead him into the kitchen, but taking in the two women, COLIN stops.)

ETHAN. In the kitchen.

COLIN. What?

(A beat.)

The air is pretty thick in here. What?

ANNA. Ask your mother. Or better yet, read this.

(She hands COLIN the letter. He reads, then looks at HESTER.)

HESTER. Jean, come and watch Ethan.

COLIN. Right, Jean's always there to save you from scenes like this. Fuck.

ETHAN. I thought we were going to the playground.

COLIN. In a minute, buddy.

JEAN. *(entering)* What is it, Hester? I'm just getting ready to go home.

HESTER. Take Ethan into the kitchen, please.

JEAN. *(taking in the severity of the situation)* Ethan, come.

(He goes with her, reluctantly. They exit.)

COLIN. So. What is there to say.

ANNA. I've told her if she sends that in she doesn't see him anymore.

*(**COLIN** looks at **ANNA**, not at all certain that is the proper threat.)*

Oh – what is this? Ready to forgive her? You still want it to be nice, don't you? In spite of all the evidence of how she is undercutting you.

COLIN. Stop it.

(A beat.)

You're uncharacteristically speechless, Hester. No defense of what you're doing here?

HESTER. I have a great deal to say, Colin, but I don't want to say it in front of her.

COLIN. Anna.

ANNA. I'm not going. What, Jean is going to watch Ethan in the kitchen, what am I supposed to do, go hide in the bathroom? No. This is about me as much as it is about you.

COLIN. It's not about you –

ANNA. I'm not leaving, okay? This is not just about the two of you.

(A beat.)

HESTER. Can I borrow your pocketbook a minute, Anna?

ANNA. What?

HESTER. Just your pocketbook.

ANNA. There's nothing in it.

HESTER. I think there is.

>(ANNA *hands it to her, in great confusion.* HESTER *opens it.*)

There they are. I was wondering where they'd gone.

COLIN. What?

HESTER. Your testicles. There they are.

ANNA. Let me have it.

HESTER. Keep them.

COLIN. Oh, this is too fucking rich.

ANNA. She doesn't respect you.

COLIN. No kidding.

ANNA. We had a fight before. She accused me of not respecting you. Look what she's willing to do to you.

HESTER. Maybe I just want to move the conversation forward. It stopped a little while ago, didn't it, for the three of us? Reagan's elected and whoosh – we're locked into a frozen state of politeness. I had a son once, we used to have good fights in this room.

COLIN. You call them good fights. Did I ever get to win them? All I wanted to do was sometimes suggest there might be a different way of looking at things. I always thought you were missing something.

HESTER. And you waited until you were almost thirty to tell me that. And you did it through her. Well come on, fight me now. Let's fight again, Colin. You are working for a loser, a Senator from New Hampshire who is going nowhere, while she rises. Am I supposed to sit here and watch that?

COLIN. Yes. This is how it plays out. You want your money back from Harvard? I've got news for you, Mother, Harvard lets in lots of mediocrities, I'm only one of them. But I am holding onto a job with this Senator, at this level, all right? And you'll kill me with this. You like that? That you're killing me?

HESTER. Of course not.

COLIN. Then tear it up.

HESTER. I can't. You know I can't.

(A beat.)

COLIN. (*turning to* **ANNA**) So what's the deal? Our ultimatum. She does this, no Ethan?

(ANNA nods.)

There it is.

HESTER. Stop.

COLIN. Shit. Mother. Look what you're forcing here.

(A beat.)

Don't you care about him?

HESTER. Don't even ask me that. This is something she's setting up. You and I could have this fight, and Ethan wouldn't be part of it. It's her who's forcing him in. Why are you going along with that?

COLIN. We're a team, that's all. We're a team.

HESTER. Don't trust her.

COLIN. What?

HESTER. I said, don't trust her. I have always said that, since you first brought her here. Be a conservative, if that's where your second rate mind – which you seem to be so proud of – is taking you. Show me it's you, though. Don't hide behind this "team" bullshit. Tell me, your mother, that it's you who would deny me my beloved grandson just for standing up for what I believe.

COLIN. Standing up for what you believe. Is that how you justify undercutting your son? I am nothing in this fight. Right?

HESTER. No.

COLIN. Then if I am something, do this for me. Tear it up and all is well.

HESTER. I don't accept these terms.

COLIN. Then I know what you're saying.

HESTER. You don't.

COLIN. I do. I really do.

HESTER. You don't, Colin.

COLIN. *(to ANNA)* Come on, we'll get him his project – he's supposed to make a little zoo with popsicle sticks. He tells me now.

(He goes off to get ERHAN.)

(HESTER and ANNA alone together a moment.)

HESTER. *(with increasing bitterness)* Thank you. Thank you for destroying everything. Thank you.

(COLIN comes in with ETHAN, holding his project.)

Ethan.

(The boy turns. She kisses him.)

(COLIN, ANNA and ETHAN start to exit.)

ETHAN. *(on his way out)* We can still go to the playground before we do this?

(They're gone. HESTER is alone for a moment, clutching the paper in her hands. JEAN enters.)

JEAN. I listened. From inside.

HESTER. Did Ethan hear?

JEAN. There is absolutely no need for you to do this, Hester. I made no promise to Colin. I can do this.

(She tries to take the letter from HESTER. HESTER holds it back.)

Hester, the Judge is likely to lose with you or without you. It is turning in our direction. Be stubborn, and you will lose your son and your grandson.

HESTER. And if he doesn't lose? If we weaken, and he squeaks by? Colin will relent, Jean.

(HESTER is making herself ready to go out.)

JEAN. You'll lose that little boy, Hester. The smell of his hair. The sound of him here – it has made a difference.

HESTER. I won't lose him. I won't lose either of them. How are we ever going to progress, Jean, if the argument for soft – love – keeps stopping us in our tracks?

JEAN. It's not soft.

(Once again **JEAN** *holds out her hand to take the letter.)*

HESTER. This is my work, not yours.

JEAN. It's both of our work, Hester.

HESTER. I'll deliver it.

(They look at each other a moment, then **HESTER** *exits.)*

*(***JEAN** *stands, watching her.)*

(Lights down.)

Scene Two

(In the dark, Barack Obama's inauguration speech, January 2009. ["There are some who question the scale of our ambitions, who suggest that our system cannot tolerate too many big plans. Their memories are short, for they have forgotten what this country has already done, what free men and women can achieve when imagination is joined to common purpose, and necessity to courage. What the cynics fail to understand is that the ground has shifted beneath them, that the stale political arguments that have consumed us for so long no longer apply."])

(The lights come up to reveal the living room substantially unchanged – a different arrangement on the table, perhaps more slipcovers, some signs that the room has not been meticulously kept up. It is the night of Barack Obama's inauguration.)

(ETHAN, now 27, is standing in the center of the room, taking in his surroundings. He's dressed in a fashionable outfit – dressed for a party, in fact. He holds in his hand an iPhone, and checks it once, nervously, for messages. Two winter coats have been laid casually on a sofa.)

DONALD. *(speaks from offstage)* This is amazing. Ethan. I can't believe these people your grandmother knew.

(DONALD enters, holding a photograph he's particularly excited by. DONALD is a young black man, roughly ETHAN's age, and dressed as fashionably.)

My God. She went to the Black and White Ball.

ETHAN. What was the Black and White Ball?

DONALD. Did you miss history altogether? It was only the party of the last century – the one Truman Capote gave after he published *In Cold Blood.*

ETHAN. Look, you better put that back, actually.

DONALD. Right. Right. Don't touch.

(DONALD exits briefly, to replace the photograph.)

ETHAN. Sorry. I'm nervous, being here.

DONALD. *(He touches* **ETHAN***'s cheek.)* I know this is hard for you. Poor pathetic boy.

ETHAN. *(trying to make light)* Right. The trauma is just waiting to get me. Right.

DONALD. You have any memories of this place at all?

ETHAN. What I remember is everyone screaming at one another. They were furious all the time.

DONALD. You'll do it. You'll just do it. Break the ice, whatever.

ETHAN. You don't need to coach me. I made this decision

(He holds his iPhone up so **DONALD** *can see and hear it.)*

Jamie sent me a clip of Michael Stipe singing "Stand" on the Washington Mall. Pretty cool, huh.? I'm bringing this back to my kids. I told them I'd bring them souvenirs from parties.

DONALD. *(going back to the photos)* Your forty kids. You fertile man.

ETHAN. Jaden. Aviva. Saoul. Look. You've got a President who looks like you.

DONALD. Sort of. Ethan, don't make too huge a deal of this. I mean he's brilliant, but –

ETHAN. How can you say that? It's not just that he's brilliant. It's going to change things. The legacy that these people handed us, all their stupid battles – over. If nothing else happens in the next four years, we are all changed by this.

DONALD. You're lecturing me on this?

ETHAN. Right. Sorry. I didn't expect, coming back here, to feel so much.

(He picks up a picture.)

Who's this?

DONALD. Henry "Scoop" Jackson. Anti-Soviet Democrat.

ETHAN. Anti-Soviet? You see what I'm talking about? Everything here, ancient battles.

DONALD. Eth, I'm a historian. I like ancient battles.

> It'll be fine, it'll be fine. You'll see this old lady, I'll ask her a couple of questions. Then we'll go dance until the cock crows.

> (**ETHAN** *smiles.*)

ETHAN. I've always liked that phrase.

> Look, however this goes down, we have to make this quick. Barack and Michelle are only going to be at these parties for like five minutes each. They're dancing to "At Last." Miss that, we miss history.

> (**DONALD** *begins singing the song as he continues to peruse the photographs. Then he turns to* **ETHAN**, *surprising him by starting to dance with him. He continues to sing as they dance.*)

DONALD. God. You're so nervous.

ETHAN. No I'm not. No.

> (**JEAN** *enters. She is in her mid-eighties now, but a healthy mid-eighties. She begins speaking before she's onstage, and when* **ETHAN** *and* **DONALD** *hear her, they break apart.*)

JEAN. She's coming, she's coming, getting herself all dolled up for you. I told her she didn't need to – oh, don't stop. You were dancing.

ETHAN. *(more embarrassed than he expected to be)* We're –

JEAN. Oh, Ethan, don't apologize. I like to see this.

> (*responding to* **ETHAN**'*s awkwardness*)

> Can I get you boys anything?

ETHAN. No, we're fine.

JEAN. Ethan, you probably don't remember, we were always terrible with food. But we've gotten better. We look at expiration dates now.

> (*A beat.*)

> You don't remember.

ETHAN. I'm sorry..

JEAN. Tell me. How did you know we'd be home?

ETHAN. We didn't. It was a chance we took.

JEAN. You told your father you were coming?

ETHAN. I asked him where you lived.

JEAN. He gave permission, then.

ETHAN. He didn't need to give permission. But, in fact, he was not keen on my coming.

JEAN. I hope we'll be seeing you more often, Ethan.

ETHAN. I live in – We live in New York.

JEAN. You're a teacher.

ETHAN. Yes. In the Bronx. And Donald's –

DONALD. A graduate student in History at Columbia.

JEAN. My.

ETHAN. We don't get down here much.

JEAN. To see your mother.

ETHAN. That's pretty much it. To see my mother.

JEAN. But tonight – ?

DONALD. *(covering for* **ETHAN**'s *silence)* We wanted to pay our (respects).

JEAN. *(ignoring* **DONALD**, *focusing on* **ETHAN**) (This) town's painful for you.

ETHAN. *(surprised by her intuition)* Yes. I didn't even tell my mother I was coming. The only thing that could get me down here this time of year was this party – parties, actually. We're invited to two. We canvassed. We went up every weekend to New Hampshire. Claremont.

(He raises his fist in a victory pump.)

JEAN. We were invited to one. Party. Not much the two of us can do anymore, two old ladies. They approached us and we gave a dinner. Raised some money. What's the name of that organization? Move – ?

DONALD. Move On? You raised money for them? That's us! That's who we worked with. You should go. You should go to the party.

JEAN. Oh, we're too old. Out into the cold on a night like this?

DONALD. No, you should. Totally.

JEAN. *(smiles)* When you're young you think you can do everything. I know. I know what we have! Do you like cognac?

(ETHAN and DONALD look at each other and shrug.)

(as JEAN moves to the drinks table:)

The last thing we had to celebrate was the vote that saved Bill Clinton from impeachment. How long ago was that?

DONALD. Ten years, I think.

JEAN. Imagine, nothing to celebrate for ten years.

(She dusts off the cognac and a set of glasses.)

(calling, off:)

Hester! These boys don't have all night!

HESTER. *(off)* Coming!

JEAN. He was here, you know. Bill Clinton. His picture is here somewhere. He came for a party. Stayed five minutes. Kind. He flirted with me. In fact, I have a dress with a little stain on it.

(They have no idea how to respond to her little joke. She hands them the cognac she's poured, pleased that she's been able to surprise them with the fact that she's still with it.)

Cognac doesn't go bad, does it?

DONALD. No. It's supposed to get better.

JEAN. *(She raises her glass.)* Ethan, Donald. Where is Hester?

(Decides to go ahead, in HESTER's absence.)

To the change in power.

(They drink. HESTER enters, at first unseen. She has indeed made some obvious attempt to "doll herself up" for this meeting.)

DONALD. *(noticing her first)* Oh. Mrs. Ferris.

*(**HESTER** and **ETHAN** stare hard at one another.)*

JEAN. Hester, you've gotten the lipstick a little wrong.

> *(She approaches **HESTER** with a tissue, but **HESTER** pushes her away, blots it herself.)*

HESTER. *(a reserve)* Ethan. All grown up.

JEAN. And this is his friend Donald, Hester.

DONALD. An honor.

JEAN. His friend. The new meaning of the word "friend".

HESTER. *(A beat. Far hipper than **JEAN** in this regard.)* What in the world is she talking about?

ETHAN. Partner is the word she's looking for, I think.

HESTER. *(She smiles.)* Maybe I always knew that.

> *(**ETHAN** and **DONALD** look at each other, confused.)*

JEAN. They're here for a party, Hester. They worked for Obama. Ethan's a teacher in New York.

HESTER. Are you?

DONALD. He won a prize last year.

ETHAN. It was nothing.

DONALD. Say it. Make your grandmother proud. Nothing to be ashamed of. A Teaching Excellence Award New York City gives to ten teachers a year. He's shy. He was responsible (for –)

ETHAN. (Stop.)

DONALD. I won't stop. The strongest class improvement in the city of New York.

ETHAN. Nothing.

DONALD. It's not nothing.

HESTER. No. Indeed not.

DONALD. And I – study this period. Your period. I'm working on my dissertation. American Liberalism in the late Vietnam years. Under Nixon-Ford. The decline of a class.

HESTER. Did we decline? I wasn't aware.

DONALD. I'm sorry. It's an academic idea. You have to have a certain boldness or nobody notices. I don't really mean decline.

HESTER. What school? Ethan.

ETHAN. It's in the Bronx. Bronx Prep, it's called. Which makes it sound like Choate for the inner city. Which it isn't. It's a name they gave the school to promote an idea. Prep. Preparation. For the future. To promote this idea that for most of these kids is just an idea – the future.

DONALD. He brings in food.

ETHAN. Stop.

DONALD. He brings in healthy food and actually feeds the kids so they can stay concentrated.

HESTER. Do you really?

ETHAN. It's something – they need. It's not a lot to do for them.

HESTER. *(looking him over carefully, but not giving much)* I'm glad to see you've done well.

ETHAN. *(allowing the cold compliment)* Thank you.

JEAN. Would you like some cognac, Hester?

HESTER. I would.

> *(JEAN brings HESTER her drink. HESTER continues to look at ETHAN. as she speaks to DONALD:)*

If you like, young man, I could show you letters. Things. Things I've kept.

DONALD. *(overwhelmed)* Original documents.

HESTER. Yes. Charting our decline. Which, given the fact that we've just inaugurated the most liberal American President since Lyndon Johnson, hardly seems (precise).

DONALD. (That was) a mistake.

HESTER. He wrote me a letter. Lyndon Johnson. During the bad days of Vietnam.

DONALD. There were good days?

HESTER. *(A small affection – at least an understanding – starting up between these two.)* During the very worst of them. Asking me if I'd host a dinner. "Where are my friends?" he asked.

DONALD. Did you host it?

HESTER. No, I didn't. Perhaps I should have, but I didn't. Lately I have come to wonder why we were so hard on poor Lyndon – Still, I have the letter. I have things I could show you.

DONALD. I could come down from New York. That would be –

HESTER. And Ethan would come, too.

(ETHAN doesn't respond.)

Though somehow I suspect Ethan disapproves of me.

ETHAN. *(deflecting)* I don't.

HESTER. *(brushing past what she actually suspects)* How is your father?

ETHAN. Good. Fine.

HESTER. He's happy on the New Hampshire Legislature?

ETHAN. I think he's found his place. He's happy with his new wife. Seems so, anyway.

HESTER. Does he ever – speak about coming down here?

ETHAN. No.

HESTER. And your mother? How is she?

ETHAN. *(smiles awkwardly)* This election wasn't very good for her.

HESTER. No. I imagine the new President will want someone else to serve as head of the National Endowment for the Humanities.

JEAN. It was never a perfect match. More cognac, anyone?

HESTER. I will have some, Jean.

JEAN. Hester, you've barely finished –

HESTER. I will have some.

(A beat.)

You know, we have worked very hard for this moment. Jean and I. For you. For you to be able to – live fully. Who sits on the Supreme Court matters. We have sacrificed a great deal for that idea. It's perhaps not fully known, not sufficiently documented. Which is why, young man, your work is important. I have something here I think you'd be interested in –

(She goes to a drawer to find the document she's looking for. As she rummages through the drawer, she takes out ETHAN's ball, where she has kept it. Is it accidental or not that she should retrieve it at this moment? She holds it up. A silent moment where she's waiting to see if he remembers.)

Do you remember this, Ethan?

JEAN. *(protective)* Hester.

HESTER. Jean, I am perfectly capable.

ETHAN. *(A beat.)* No. I don't.

(She puts it away.)

HESTER. No reason you should.

DONALD. *(on pins and needles)* You were going to show me something –

HESTER. Tell me, Ethan. Let's cut the crap, if you'll forgive an old lady using such language. Enough – beating around the bush. Why did you come here tonight?

ETHAN. We were here. I knew I had a grandmother. I thought –

DONALD. *(finishing for him)* It was time.

ETHAN. I can answer, thank you. My father has never told me why you two stopped speaking.

*(**DONALD** has a quiet reaction to this.)*

HESTER. A very small argument. One we never should have had. But we did. And it led to a larger one we could never find our way out of. Sacrifices had to be made in those days. It's hard to see how every small thing mattered in order to come to this moment, but it did.

ETHAN. What mattered, coming to this moment – *I* think –

(a harshness coming in; it makes the words difficult for him to get out)

– was – bodies on the ground. Doors knocked on. Talking to people, one on one, out there in the world. That's what mattered. Your old battles are a distraction at this point. Didn't you hear the President's speech today?

HESTER. Yes, apparently the past doesn't count anymore. The old knock down, drag out fights that made this moment possible, insignificant, apparently. Your friend ought to be able to straighten you out on the truth of that. If you think having elected a black President, all our battles are over, think again.

ETHAN. You talk about fights but it seems more like entrenched positions you didn't know how to get yourselves out of.

HESTER. And you will do better. No doubt.

ETHAN. We hope to.

HESTER. Find a way to force change without breaking a single heart or severing a single relationship. Best of luck.

ETHAN. I'm sorry.

HESTER. Don't apologize. Fight. It's good to fight. Fights are what I miss.

You'll marry, you two?

ETHAN. We talk about it.

HESTER. Good. You should. That's what it's been about. Our entrenched positions. Our distracting old battles. One of the things it's been about. All right. Go to your party. I know you're anxious.

DONALD. We wanted to pay our respects.

HESTER. Which you have.

DONALD. And. If I could come see those letters.

HESTER. Any time. Only one promise.

DONALD. Of course.

HESTER. In your title. Leave out the word "decline".

DONALD. Done.

HESTER. I've always preferred the word "ascend".

(*looking carefully at him*)

Even when I'm not the one ascending.

DONALD. (*A beat.*) Done.

HESTER. And Ethan will come sometime.

DONALD. I'll have to drag him. He works all weekend. He didn't win a prize for nothing.

ETHAN. I'm not sure I can do that.

HESTER. So this is to be it then. All right. Now you know you have a grandmother. That's enough for you, is it? Go to your party.

(**ETHAN** *and* **DONALD** *start putting on their coats.*)

And we'll come.

DONALD. Yes!

JEAN. Hester, it's a freezing night.

HESTER. We have coats. We have furs from the days when it was still all right to wear them. We'll go out and be embarrassments. Will anyone remember us? Will anyone remember – ? Jean, what did we do with the invitation?

JEAN. In a drawer somewhere.

HESTER. Look for it, Jean.

JEAN. (*She begins reluctantly looking through drawers, which are packed with useless things.*) I still think it's a bad idea.

HESTER. Ethan, there's a closet just outside there.

(**ETHAN** *looks at her. Something is going on with him. She picks up on it.*)

You don't want us to come.

(*A beat.*)

Get us our coats, please.

*(He hesitates a moment, then goes. **HESTER** looks after him.)*

JEAN. Why do we have coupons for toilet paper that expired when Bush One was President?

HESTER. Because we're silly. We're silly. We're just silly, but we're going to a party, Jean. We're going to celebrate this moment. Because we owe it to ourselves. Oh never mind, never mind. Just find it.

*(She takes out a drawer and dumps it out. At the bottom, a large white envelope. **DONALD** saves it.)*

DONALD. Here. This is what the invitations look like.

HESTER. *(opening it)* Yes. Jean.

(A look between the two sisters. An understanding.)

JEAN. You'll find us a cab, young man.

DONALD. Of course I will.

(He exits.)

JEAN. Oh God, has anything really changed, Hester? I'm still sending a black man out for a cab.

*(**ETHAN** comes on with two fur coats.)*

ETHAN. Are these the ones you meant?

HESTER. *(putting hers on, as **JEAN** does hers)* If we wear these, we might get shot.

JEAN. Hester, we can't. We have coats, for God's sake.

*(**JEAN** is about to start off to find their regular winter coats.)*

ETHAN. No. Wear them. Come with us.

(A beat.)

I wasn't telling the truth before, about not knowing. I was – maybe foolishly – testing you. My father told me. Why you two stopped speaking. And I was – afraid to come here.

HESTER. Afraid?

JEAN. *(A moment of protectiveness. She adjusts her own coat, then* HESTER*'s.)* I'll make sure that young man knows where to look.

ETHAN. *(correcting her)* Donald.

JEAN. Donald.

(She exits.)

*(*HESTER *and* ETHAN *alone together.)*

ETHAN. Afraid. And angry. He always told me you rejected me. Rejected both of us. For an idea. That's how the story came down to me.

HESTER. It was not simply an idea. And I did not want to reject you. There was no need to reject you.

ETHAN. But you did.

(He smiles self-consciously, instinctively deflecting the heaviness of what he's accusing her of.)

HESTER. Ethan, perhaps your parents never told you there was a time when I tried. More times than one. To resume a relationship –

ETHAN. He told me that. Look, I'm a little embarrassed to be having this argument with someone I *(barely know)*.

HESTER. (After your) parents' divorce, I tried even harder.

ETHAN. *(by now realizing that the actual confrontation is unavoidable)* The damage was done. He told me. By then. It was too difficult for both of you. You gave up. You both gave up.

(She doesn't answer.)

Which always left me wondering. How you could have done that. You fight for things, but you don't lose people.

HESTER. Sometimes you do. And years go by, you pretend the idea was all that mattered. You justify yourself because of the idea. And then you meet the person you missed knowing.

I did not want to see you. I thought it would be easier not seeing you.

(A beat.)

HESTER. *(cont.)* Marry, Ethan. That's what all the wreckage was for. So that change would come. It's the only justification. Would you trade the rights we won you just so that the two of us could have gone on?

(He goes to the drawer where the ball is kept. He takes the ball out, bounces it, catches it, looks at her. Then he puts the ball back inside and closes the drawer. Slowly, she puts out her arm.)

(He hesitates a moment, then takes her arm. They start off, but she stops. They look at each other a moment.)

(Then they exit together.)

(Lights down. End of play.)